A POCKETFUL OF $20s

Charleston, SC
www.PalmettoPublishing.com

A Pocketful of $20s
Copyright © 2020 by Madelaine Lawrence

First Edition

ISBN-13: 978-1-64990-543-7
ISBN-10: 1-64990-543-2

Best wishes,
Madelaine Lawrence

A
Pocketful
of
20

By Madelaine Lawrence

1

Lynn and Allan

As Dickens once said, it was the best of times; it was the worst of times. That's how Lynn Price describes her life. She enjoys being the nursing director of the emergency department in Deer Park, North Carolina. It is a busy ED, but Lynn, her staff, and the doctors help many people and fail exceptionally few. She has close ties with her family, consisting of her mother, Dorothy; her brother, George and his wife, Angie; two nephews, Bernie and Edison, and a niece, Eloise. It is the men in her life, currently, Alan Johnson, who create the worst of times.

"Don't tell me you are doing that again?" said Alan, this morning. His irritation showed in his pursed lips and ruffled forehead, making him look more worked up than usual.

"Yes, dear. I'm going to do that again. I promised my mother, during the holiday season, I would find five people who were struggling and give them a twenty-dollar bill like she used to do." Lynn's usual facial expression was one of kindness and attentiveness. Defiance now filled her face making her look steadfast.

"I'm off to the bank for my five twenty-dollar bills," she answered. "Don't tell me you are going to start complaining about me handing out the money again." Lynn pushed her long, dark, wavy hair behind her neck to allow the flap from her knitted cap to cover her ears. She had been putting on her warm coat, anticipating a chilly blast of winter.

These arguments left her exhausted. She wanted to be happy today. She often wondered how she could be successful in school and at work, and have a wonderful family, but screw up so badly in her relationships with men.

Alan huffed a little. He stood up from his chair as tall as he could make his six-foot frame stretch. "I can't stand that you give good money out to these people. They need to get off their lazy butts and get a decent job!" said Alan.

"Oh, oh, I can tell by the look on your face, you are upset with me now. Sorry about that. I'm off to work," Alan said, grabbing his coat. "Wait! I'll walk out with you."

She and Alan saw the world so differently. There was no reconciling their views even though they tried during the last six months of living together. Day in and day out, Lynn's ED had patients that feared they would fall off the financial edge on which they lived. She felt for them. She knew twenty dollars wasn't much money but maybe enough to buy something unaffordable at that moment. Alan, on the other hand, sold expensive real estate to people with high incomes. He admired their lifestyles—people with marginal incomes were just people who sat on their porches collecting welfare checks.

They took the elevator from their apartment to the main floor. Alan kissed her goodbye as if no argument had passed between them.

His parting words were, "See you later, and remember you could work your way to being a vice president at the hospital instead of spending time with people who are just too lazy to work hard enough." He turned and walked away down the street.

A VP? Why would I want that job? Lynn thought. *They never see patients. Where's the satisfaction in that?*

The warm sun made the forty-eight-degree weather seem almost pleasant to Lynn. The stores already had Christmas and Hanukkah decorations up. It was an enjoyable walk to the bank from which she exited with her five twenty-dollar bills. These bills would go to men or women, young or old, who Lynn could see were in low-income jobs or making careful decisions about spending the dollars they had.

One time she and her mother, Dorothy, were in a store connected to a gas station. They were behind a young man at the checkout counter, who looked to be in his late teens, early twenties. He was paying for his gas with cash. His bill came to six dollars.

"But I only put five dollars' worth into my car, according to the meter outside, and five dollars is all I have," he replied. "I'm trying to get home from school."

"You better start looking for change to make up the extra one dollar," the man behind the counter responded. Lynn handed the man a dollar bill, and he rang his register and cleared the charge. Lynn stayed in line to pay her bill. Dorothy stopped the young man and pressed a twenty in his hand. "You drive safely home, and have a wonderful holiday with your family," she told him.

"No, no, I can't take your money," the young man said in protest.

"I have a son besides my daughter," Dorothy said, pointing to Lynn. "He used to drive home from school pretty much penniless. One day, someone gave him an extra ten dollars. I'm returning that favor ... and it's a twenty-dollar bill because of inflation."

"Thank you," said the young man. "I know my mother would thank you, too, if she were here." He gave Dorothy a hug and a smile that made her day.

Lynn's mother had donated to various charities, particularly at Christmas. Lynn knew she would have liked a little more of a connection with the recipients and maybe helped them a little more. One day her mother thought about giving out these twenty-dollar bills. At least she could see the people to whom she was giving the money.

Her mother remembered living with no extra cash. "There was the day when I drove to a meeting with three dollars in my wallet. I had to go over a toll bridge and was panicked that maybe I did not have enough money to pay the toll," her mother had told her once. "After Dad and I divorced, it was tough. A twenty-dollar bill then would have been very welcome." Lynn knew her father did not give her mother child support money for her and her brother regularly. There were several grilled cheese and tomato soup dinners those months.

Lynn knew some of her ED patients had been on that type of financial precipice. One man told her sometimes he had to choose between buying his insulin for his diabetes or his blood pressure meds. She was so shocked that she blurted out, "But you need both of them." The man had told her occasionally he could not afford both. Sometimes he would buy the insulin and break his blood pressure meds in half to last longer. Lynn shook her head and hoped the social worker she referred him to would help him pay for all his meds.

But today was Lynn's day off from work. She was going Christmas shopping for her two nephews and her niece. It was to be a fun day.

2

The Toy Store

THE TOY STORE IN DOWNTOWN DEER PARK HAD A WARM, welcoming feeling. Children were sitting in the small nooks with kid size tables and chairs and puzzles laid out for them. Every section had a different theme, from books and puzzles to stuffed animals and construction toys. Her eight-year-old nephew, Bernie, was into Lego construction toys. The taller the building, the better. Her brother, George, had given her a list of the kits he already had.

There were several kits for building skyscrapers, but many were for older kids. She had a budget of fifty dollars for each child with some flexibility. This year Lynn was set on buying everyone the same number of Christmas presents.

Last year she had bought Bernie an expensive set with a remote-controlled construction crane and a truck. She ended up getting Edison and Eloise less costly toys but more of them to add up to fifty dollars. Bernie wanted to know how come his sister and brother got more presents than him. When she tried to explain his gift was more expensive, it did not satisfy him.

Lost in her thought processes, Lynn reached for a box, not realizing the woman next to her was also reaching for it.

"So sorry," said the woman.

"It was my fault," said Lynn. "I was so into thinking about what to get my nephew that I did not see you."

"It's so hard to know what would be special for kids these days," the woman said.

Lynn looked carefully at the woman. She was small, maybe five feet four inches, in her early thirties. She was dressed nicely, on the thin side, but with a heavier sweater instead of a coat.

"Who are you looking to buy a present for?" asked Lynn.

"Something for my son, who is seven," the woman responded. "He's such a good kid. I'd like to get him something special."

"My nephew is eight now, but last year when he was seven, he loved this construction set with the remote-control crane," Lynn said, showing the woman the box.

"I know David would love that set," the woman said. "But thirty dollars plus tax is too expensive for me. I'm looking at the ten and fifteen-dollar kits. Were there any in that price range your nephew liked when he was seven?" she asked. "My name is Theresa, by the way."

"I'm Lynn."

Lynn knew she had met her first twenty-dollar recipient for this season. She thought about asking her what kind of work she did to be sure but believed that would be too intrusive. Lynn had found the tricky part was giving the twenty dollars to someone who was not doing a service for her. It was easy to tip a waitress extra or someone who cleaned restrooms. Lynn had learned that handing a stranger a twenty-dollar bill took a little more finessing. People were sensitive to receiving what they perceived as charity.

"I tell you what," said Lynn. "Besides picking out Christmas presents, I'm on a mission to help my mother. She's older now with a heart condition and cannot walk around like she used to. The greatest joy she had at Christmas was giving a twenty-dollar bill to five people who could use the money to buy something a little special. I'd like you to be the first recipient of the Pocket Full of Twenties Club. Would you help me make my mother happy by taking this twenty-dollar bill?"

Lynn held out the twenty-dollar bill to Theresa.

"I don't know what to say."

"Saying yes would be great. My mother will be delighted to know about David and his construction kit. It would help me out a lot, too," said Lynn.

"I guess it's okay if I help you out," Theresa said. "Thank you, and thank your mom."

After hugging Lynn, Theresa took the construction kit off the shelf and headed toward the checkout line with the twenty-dollar bill tucked in her hand.

Lynn wanted to offer Theresa her coat but figured that would be too much.

Back to finding a gift for Bernie, she said to herself. She was happy with her choice for the first recipient, but at the same time, she wished she could know more about Theresa and how David ended up liking his construction kit.

3

Theresa and Daniel

THERESA WALKED HOME AS FAST AS SHE COULD. IT WAS ALmost time for her to go to work. Her boss at the *Sea Grill* agreed to have her serve lunch but warned, "You better be here on time every day."

Her apartment was nearby. She had just enough time to hide David's Christmas present and catch the bus to work. She smiled all the way home. Last year they had no extra money for toys. She had wrapped up clothes she had bought David at the discount store. He was disappointed, of course. At six, he had the wisdom of a grown man. He said, "Mom and Dad, I know things are hard. Thanks for buying these clothes for me." Tears welled in Theresa's eyes when he said those words.

"Our luck is finally changing," she thought. They had moved to Deer Park, North Carolina, barely a year ago. It was a gamble that paid off.

Daniel, her husband, had been a long-distance trucker in Wisconsin. The pay at his company was lower than in other areas. Driving in the winter was also more hazardous. Theresa thought back to the conversation they had the night they decided to move.

"You look exhausted," said Theresa to her husband. His eyes lacked any spark, and his shoulders slumped. Theresa missed the enthusiastic greetings she used to get when he came home.

"I don't know how much longer I'm going to be able to do this," said Daniel. "I had a bad skid on I-94 and almost jackknifed. It was terrifying. The roads are so dangerous in the winter."

"Let's move," Theresa said emphatically.

"Really?" asked Daniel.

"Why not? We don't have any family here anymore, and the weather is terrible. The pay isn't the best. We need to enjoy our lives more. We can move to someplace warmer and more hospitable."

Daniel looked at Theresa in amazement. "You think it would be that easy? What about the house?"

"Sell it," exclaimed Theresa.

"What about our stuff?" questioned Daniel.

"Throw out most of it. Move the rest. I looked online while at the library, and truckers are in demand all over. They might even be willing to pay to move our stuff." Theresa was getting more excited as she said all this. "You know, Daniel, we are living paycheck to paycheck here. We can't get ahead."

"Have you been talking with your sister?" asked Daniel a little suspiciously with just a hint of laughter in his voice.

"Yes, I have! It's been an eye-opening conversation. Life is better in Deer Park, North Carolina. Hardly ever any snow. There are beaches to visit on hot summer days. David would love that. AND truckers get paid more."

"What? How do you know that?"

"Louisa looked it up online. There are local trucking companies offering lots of jobs. Most pay over $60,000 a year with health insurance, a 401K, and one even has tuition reimbursement if you want to go to school. Another company had a sign-on bonus. We can go to the library and check them out on the computer there."

"What's a 401K again?" asked Daniel.

"I asked Louisa that. She said it's a retirement fund. You don't have one now because the company lists you as an independent contractor. If you are considered an employee of a trucking company, the owner puts money into this fund, and you can put money in, too, for when you retire. Right now, we have no extra money. Our health insurance is the cheapest there is. We have no security if anything happens to either of us. We can do better."

"I can tell you and Louisa have been working a lot on this. I'm glad you two included me in the move and had not planned to leave me behind," said Daniel smiling broadly. Theresa gave him a gentle hit with her dishtowel.

"You know I would not do anything without taking you with me. Besides, Eric Mabius hasn't shown up on the doorstep yet," she said, teasing.

"He would be here in a minute if he knew you," replied Daniel bringing Theresa close to him. They kissed softly.

Theresa did not bring up her working part-time to Daniel. She had asked Louisa about local restaurants. She also had Louisa check on their house's selling price and check on housing in Deer Park.

The next day, Daniel came into the kitchen and said, "Let's do it. Let's move."

Theresa and Daniel hugged, and the rest, as they say, was history. They used the sign-on bonus from Daniel's new job to move to Deer Park. He got a ten thousand dollar a year raise with health insurance and the 401K. They sold their house and put away the ten thousand dollars they had earned after paying off the mortgage and the realtor. The plan was to rent an apartment first and then save enough money to buy a house where they wanted to live.

It's coming together, thought Theresa. *Now, this extra twenty dollars was a sign that we are in the right place. Daniel will be pleased to hear about this contribution to our new life.*

4

Theresa and David

THE NEXT MORNING AFTER DANIEL LEFT FOR WORK, THERESA started making pancakes with chocolate chips for David. She felt a celebration was in order. The aroma from the kitchen reached David's bedroom. He woke up quickly and ran to the kitchen.

"Mom, what are you making?" he asked. Theresa generally reserved chocolate chip pancakes for Sunday morning. "Are we celebrating something?" David asked.

"Yes, my young man, we are celebrating our new life. It's turning out fine."

"Did something else good happen? Was Aunt Louisa on the phone?"

Theresa debated if she should tell David about the twenty-dollar bill she got while in the toy store. Maybe it would get him a little excited about Christmas. David talked truly little about the holidays, except for the play at his school. David knew they were going to get together with Louisa and her family on Christmas day. He was happy about that. He might be worried it will be more clothes for Christmas.

Theresa had told Daniel about the twenty dollars last night. At first, he was unhappy, considering it to be charity. When she explained the woman was doing it for her mother and it would help her out, Daniel was okay with accepting it. He thought they might even have enough money to buy David another smaller gift.

"Sit down for your pancakes, and I'll tell you another reason we are celebrating," said Theresa.

David sat across from his mother at the island in the kitchen, their established ritual for breakfast on school days. It was a few moments every day, filled with warmth and closeness for both of them.

"Yesterday, David, I was in the toy store downtown." David's blue eyes opened a little wider.

"Yes?"

"I was looking for something for you for Christmas."

"In the toy store?" David checked.

"There was a lady in the store also looking for a toy for her nephew. We chatted about what were good toys for you two. Her nephew is a little older than you. She showed me something he liked at your age."

"What was it? Did you think I'd like it?" asked David, who had stopped eating. He was now intent on his mother's words.

"I did think you would like what she showed me," Theresa responded. "It was a little expensive, which is what I told the lady."

"Oh," said David, focusing on eating again instead of listening to his mother.

"This lady said she was on a mission. Do you know what a mission is?"

David thought. "Like a mission into space?"

"Yes, that's one type of mission. Sometimes it is when a person wants to do something to help someone else."

"People can have bad missions, too, that hurt people, right?" asked David.

Theresa thought sometime later, she and David will need to talk about where he's seen people with bad missions. Maybe some of the television shows he watches aren't the best.

"This lady was on a good mission. She told me her mother used to hand twenty-dollar bills to five people right before Christmas. Her mother no longer has the energy to hand out the twenty-dollar bills and asked this daughter to do it for her. She would look for people that could use a little bonus at Christmastime."

"Like us?"

"Sort of, although our lives are better now living here. Don't you think?"

David thought about it. He missed some of his friends in Wisconsin but now had new friends. His bus ride to school was so much shorter, so he could sleep longer. His school had a great play area, and now this holiday play. He could tell his mom and dad were happier. *Yep*, he thought *life was better.*

"Yep, life is good here." He smiled. His Aunt Louisa had given him a Life Is Good t-shirt, and he liked the saying.

"When I told this lady in the toy store that while the toy she had found was wonderful, it was beyond my budget, she asked me a question," said Theresa.

"What question?"

"Could she give me twenty dollars to help her complete the mission her mother had sent her on?"

"What did you say?"

"At first, I hesitated, but when she insisted that I was helping her out, I accepted the twenty dollars."

Hoping against hope for the answer he wanted to hear, David asked, "What did you do with it?"

Theresa smiled. "What do you think I did?"

"I don't know. Tell me!" David was now as focused as a puppy waiting for a treat.

"I bought you the present the lady said her nephew liked so much," said Theresa.

David ran over to his mother and gave her a big hug. He was so excited, he started dancing around the kitchen.

"So, what is this gift you bought for me?" asked David when he stopped swirling.

"You will know on Christmas Eve," said Theresa giving David's head a rub.

Theresa was happy. *Life is definitely good*, she thought. *Let's hope it keeps up*!

5

Lynn and Alan

Lynn walked back into her three-bedroom apartment she shared with Alan. He had insisted they could afford the twenty-five hundred dollars a month rent. Lynn had to admit, the layout and location of the apartment were ideal. She could walk and bike easily to the beach. As soon as she saw the Intracoastal Waterway and marshes, this feeling of relaxation and joy came over her. The beach and marsh views were incredible, changing all day, and visible from their deck. There was also a twenty-four-hour fitness center and a swimming pool downstairs. Lynn initially had wanted to buy a house, but Alan had talked her out of it.

"Maybe we will buy a house when we get married," he had said. That was a year ago. They never discussed marriage plans after that.

"Anyone home?" Alan called out as he entered the hallway. Even though she and Alan didn't have similar values, there was chemistry between them. Lynn could feel that chemistry watching the muscles in his back ripple as he removed his coat and seeing his seductive blue eyes look her way.

"Hi, dear. I'm in the kitchen."

"Love seeing you in the kitchen when I come home from work," responded Alan. "What's for dinner?" he asked, squeezing Lynn on her shoulder.

"We have curried chicken with rice and a side salad. Are you ready for your cocktail?"

"I'll get it, sweetie. What would you like?"

"I'll have a glass of merlot, thanks."

"You know white wine, or maybe a rose is better with chicken."

"I'm fine with the merlot. I like the fruity taste and smooth finish." *Oh, here we go with the pairing of wine and food. I am going to try to ignore the comment*, she resolved.

Alan left for the bedroom to change his clothes. He neglected to pour her a glass of wine. She saw that he had fixed his martini. It was a reminder that she needed to be more sophisticated in what wine she chose. They had the same differences of opinion with jewelry. Her skin tones called for white gold or silver-colored jewelry. Alan thought gold jewelry should be gold-colored and was more elegant and more luxurious looking. Jewelry gifts from him were always yellow gold. White gold didn't work because others couldn't tell the jewelry was really a different gold color and not just silver.

As these thoughts ran through Lynn's head, she began to think more about the pluses and minuses of her life with Alan. The putdowns were making her angry now, but they had worked out a consistent schedule for their lives. Alan thought most people just needed to work harder to make it in life, but Lynn thought people needed help from time to time. She trusted Alan to be faithful to her, no small plus given he was a good looking, successful guy.

"So, how was your day, Alan?" Lynn asked when Alan entered the kitchen.

"It was great. I got an offer on a seven-hundred-thousand-dollar beachfront property. It's too bad I have to split the commission with the realtor who listed the property and the agency. But it still will be a nice payoff of about twelve thousand dollars to me. We can pay the rent again this month."

"Congratulations. Good for you."

"No, good for us. I was thinking it might be time to think about buying a house. This place is great but a financial loser. No return on the money we spend."

"I'm good with that idea," said Lynn. She was wondering if getting married was going to be part of that plan. Lynn wanted to have at least two children. So far, Alan resisted that idea.

"Great. I'll check on houses we might like and can afford."

Lynn poured her glass of merlot. Anger built up in her as she did so.

"How was your day off today? Any good finds?"

"It was great. The weather was beautiful. I took a run on the beach and then did a little Christmas shopping."

"Please don't get me any more ties. I have more than enough and like to pick out my own that go with my business look."

Lynn thought, *Your business look—stuffy and arrogant.*

"I went to the toy store looking for something for little Bernie. While I was there, I found a woman who could use a twenty-dollar bill."

"So, you are doing that again. When are you going to realize these people are just a bunch of takers?" said Alan. His voice was loud, with an edge of anger.

"You know I promised my mother I would do this. She'll be excited to hear what happened even though you are not."

"You are right. I don't want to hear about handouts to takers. Is supper ready? I'm starving."

Dinner was quiet. Alan said the dinner was tasty and thanked her for the meal. He then retired to the den, where he kept his computer and papers. Lynn sat on the deck, drinking her glass of merlot while contemplating her personal life. There were pluses: a stable relationship, financial security, and companionship. Besides not liking the comments about her apparent lack of sophistication, what else was wrong?

6

Lynn and Dr. Peter

LYNN WAS UP EARLY THE NEXT DAY TO GET TO WORK ON TIME. Alan was still asleep when she left for work, for which she was grateful. In the car, her thoughts switched to work. She needed to check the staffing plan for the next three months and go over the supply list.

She secured her purse in her office and hung up her coat. As was her practice, she went out to check on the staff and the patients. Every day was a new adventure—she loved that part of her job. This ED had twenty patient rooms and a trauma room, designated as a Level II Trauma Center. They one day hoped to be a Level I Trauma Center. The hospital needed to have a full-blown cardiac surgery program for that to happen.

The night staff report indicated a car accident resulting in one person with a severe head injury and another with a fractured tibia. The nurses called the neurosurgeon and orthopedic doctors, who came immediately. The patient with the leg fracture was in surgery, and the patient with the head injury was in the ICU.

The department was quiet this morning. One patient was having an asthmatic attack, and another one had chest pain. They were both stable after being treated.

Her head buried into her paperwork; she lifted her head in response to a knock on the door. It was Dr. Peter Fry, the chief of orthopedics in the hospital, with two cups of coffee in his hand.

"Thought you could use a pick-me-up," he said, smiling. "Black with one sugar for you."

He took a seat in one of the chairs in front of her desk.

"So how goes the war?" he asked.

"I should be asking you that question. I see you were on call for the patient with the fractured tibia. How did that go?"

"He's all patched up, resting comfortably on the ortho floor. Your staff, by the way, were great. How did they get to be so efficient?"

"I only hire and keep the best," Lynn said, smiling back at Peter.

"I think it's good management, myself," he said, winking at Lynn.

"You just like flattering me so you can come and hide out in my office," she said back. "I saw the VPs walking around. Bill from finance was looking for you."

"Not surprising. I delivered my preliminary budget to the CFO. Which reminds me, I hear there's a new Mexican restaurant at the beach with great food. Don't we need to meet to go over the budget for the new splint systems?" Peter asked with slight pleading in his voice.

"You know, I just wrote something about meeting with you about all those new systems," Lynn said, rifling through the papers on her desk, pretending to find something. "I don't want the staff to get their hopes up that we might be getting them. A Mexican restaurant sounds like the right place and the right time to do that."

"Meet you there at seven on Thursday? I'll text you the address."

"Sounds great. Looking forward to it," replied Lynn.

Peter looked at her and smiled. He waved goodbye as he walked out of her office.

She always felt good when Peter stopped in. She was beginning to realize her unhappiness with Alan might have something to do with how pleasantly people at work, like Peter, treated her. There were no smug deprecating comments, mostly compliments. Peter did not hesitate to deal with patient treatment problems in the ED, but he did it constructively, like a good friend.

7

Lynn, Dorothy, and George

On her way home from work, Lynn stopped to have dinner with her mother, Dorothy, who now lived in a two-bedroom apartment that was part of a multisystem living center for the elderly. The building's entrance featured high ceilings, a luxurious chandelier, marble floors, and a key fob operated elevator. Only those who lived there and one extra family member had a fob.

"Hi, Mom," said Lynn. "Every time I enter the lobby, I think I want to live here. How's it going with you?"

"I agree this place defies the definition of the 'old folks' home.'" Dorothy laughed and hugged her daughter. "I took the liberty of ordering dinner in for us. It's always such a treat to have you here."

Dorothy took a seat on her couch and tapped the cushion next to Lynn to sit down. "How are you?" she asked. "You said you managed to give away a twenty-dollar bill. Tell me about it."

Lynn described her encounter with Theresa in the toy store. Dorothy smiled through the entire telling of the event.

"Thank you so much for doing this. My heart can't handle that much walking anymore. Thank goodness for this lovely apartment."

Lynn knew her mother's ejection fraction, a percentage of how much blood gets pumped out with each heart contraction was forty-two percent. That made her heart function borderline low and at risk for heart failure.

"Mom, you know how much I love handing out these twenty-dollar bills."

Lynn got up to answer the doorbell. The supper was on the delivery cart. It was chicken frittata with mushroom risotto and fresh green beans with warm biscuits. The dessert was covered up and placed on the kitchen counter. Dorothy had set the table so the server, Dorika, could set the dishes down easily.

"Lynn, how are you doing?" Dorothy asked when settled at the table. "It seems something is bothering you."

"It's Alan. His comments about me not meeting up to the standards he has in his head are getting to me. It's hard to know what to do. I wish we got along as well as you and Dad did," said Lynn.

"Don't fool yourself into thinking Dad and I never had some rough times. There were a few times I thought about leaving him," Dorothy explained.

"Wow! I never knew that. You two looked like the perfect couple. You always seemed so happy together," said Lynn.

"I never told you or your brother about the other woman in your dad's life. Nothing very significant happened between them, but it was close," Dorothy said.

Lynn felt she was sitting there with her mouth open. Her father involved with another woman? Holy smokes!

"Have you sat down and had a heart-to-heart talk with Alan? He's the one who needs to know how you are feeling. That's what finally helped Dad and me through the tough times," said Dorothy.

Before she could respond, the doorbell rang again. Lynn opened the door to let in her brother, George.

"It's so good to see you," said Lynn, hugging George. "Didn't know you were coming."

"Fortunately, Mom did and gave the henchmen at the front desk the heads up. I said no to dinner but yes to dessert and seeing two of my favorite women. So, what did I miss?" asked George.

George walked over to kiss his mother. "Good to see you, dear. We were just talking about Alan."

"That pompous fool! You mean you haven't gotten rid of him yet, Lynn?"

"We know where you stand, George," laughed Lynn.

"Now come on. You know what a snob he is. He thinks he is so superior because he sells upscale houses. He doesn't own them—he puts them up for sale. Give me a break about his comments about *pairing* wine with food. Trust me. I'm good with the wine experts who know what wine should go with what food. The problem with Alan is he acts like he is the guru of wine pairing."

George stood up with his chest out and a dish towel over his arm, holding a bottle of wine. "And you know you are scum if you don't follow my suggestions," he said, pretending to scrape the scum off his shoes.

By now, Lynn was hysterically laughing. As the CEO of a pharmaceutical product development company, George has contacts with successful people daily. Yet, he talked to his employees the same way he spoke to any high ranking official or investor.

"Mostly, though, I don't like how he treats you, Lynn. You are a smart, beautiful woman with a heart as big as all outdoors. You deserve someone who tells you that every day," he said, hugging Lynn.

"Let's have dessert," offered Dorothy, also with a big smile on her face. She uncovered the key lime pie with pecan pralines, berries, and berry coulis.

"So, what wine pairing should we have with this dessert?" asked George with his pinky finger up in the air as he took his first bite.

Lynn gave him a soft sock to his shoulder. "Mom, she's hitting me," George complained to Dorothy.

Dorothy smiled at her two children. "You better behave, or I'll send you both to your rooms!" she replied, pretending to take their complaints seriously.

8

Lynn and Dorika

Just as Lynn was putting her coat on, the doorbell rang again. It was Dorika there to pick up the dishes. Lynn still thought they should have places like this for working couples. She was sure people with children would be especially delighted with this type of service.

"Bye, Mom," said Lynn hugging her mother. She held the door open for Dorika, enabling her to push her cart out the door. It occurred to her that Dorika might be able to use a twenty-dollar bill.

The hallway was empty when Lynn stopped Dorika from going further down the hall. "Dorika, I so appreciate how kind you are to my mother. I know you do services beyond delivering food and picking up dishes for her. Here's a little something for you. I hope you have a wonderful holiday."

Lynn handed Dorika the twenty-dollar bill. As Dorika reached out to accept the gift, Lynn noticed a bruise on Dorika's arm. It looked to Lynn like fingertips seen in 'grab mark' contusions. As a nurse in the

ED, she always considered fingertip bruising as a possible sign of domestic violence.

"Dorika, is anyone hurting you?" she asked.

"No, no. I am clumsy. I dropped a tray on my arm," Dorika replied. "Thank you, Miss Lynn, for my gift. You are so ... so ... how you say?" She held her hands out in an outstretched, giving pose.

"You are very welcome. We appreciate all you do. If you ever need something I can help with, call me," Lynn said, handing Dorika her card. She hugged her and thought she felt a slight tensing as if the embrace had caused Dorika pain. She was more confident now someone was abusing Dorika. Lynn planned on checking the ED records in the morning for visits by Dorika because of injuries. All she knew about Dorika was that she was from Hungary. She was married to a Hungarian, but they did not have any children.

One of the worse domestic abuse cases Lynn had seen was the wife of a prominent businessman. He would come home drunk, drag his wife out of bed, and throw her against the wall in their bedroom. She kept denying her husband abused her. The last time this wife came into the ED, she was unconscious because of head injuries. Lynn and her staff could not convince the woman to seek help when she had come in before, even though plenty was available. That was a failure for Lynn. The social worker said it was not an unusual response from an abused patient. In that case, the woman had a beautiful house, a new car, and a community status. She tolerated the abuse for those perks.

Lynn knew she could help Dorika or at least provide her with some support. She called Detective Stan Gregowski on her way home. She and Stan lived in the same neighborhood as kids. Stan was older but had a sister her age, so Lynn knew him and his family. She and Stan had also worked together to help abused and trafficked women who came to the ED. She was hoping he might have some advice about Dorika.

"Detective Gregowski. How can I help you?" answered Stan when Lynn called from work the next day.

"Hi, Stan, it's Lynn Price. I'm sure hoping you can help me."

"Hi, Lynn, good to hear from you. I would love to chat, but I'm on my way out the door. Can we talk tomorrow? My office? Your office? Lunch?"

"If it's okay with you, lunch will be the best. It's not about a patient—at least not yet. I could use your advice."

"How about one o'clock at the *Sea Grill*?" said Stan.

"Perfect. See you then." Lynn hung up her phone, relieved. *Thank goodness for Stan*, she thought. It dawned on her she was having lunch and dinner with two different men this week. It was a revelation realizing she enjoyed being with both of these men more than being with Alan.

DORIKA LOOKED AT THE BILL MISS LYNN HAD GIVEN HER when she was on the elevator. *Wow*, she thought. *Twenty dollars. Where can I hide it so Ambrus won't find it until I bury it with the rest?* She decided to hide the money in her sock under the sole of her foot.

On the bus ride home, all Dorika could think about was what to do with the money. *Now, with this money, I have four hundred dollars. I can take a long bus ride, but then what? Where to go?*

"Where have you been?" asked Ambrus as Dorika entered their apartment." I was getting worried about you." He gave Dorika a gentle kiss on the check.

"It was just a busy day today," said Dorika. She was delighted Ambrus was in a good mood. She would do her best not to say anything to set him off.

"Too many of the male patients flirting with you?" he asked.

"They are a little old and weak to do too much flirting. Besides, you know I only have eyes for you," Dorika replied, giving Ambrus a hug and a kiss. "What are you making for dinner?" She was hoping Ambrus had gotten off his jealousy track.

"We will be having spaghetti and meatballs with a salad and a glass of wine. You have time for a shower if you want."

Dorika was relieved. She knew after three years of living with Ambrus, suggesting she take a shower was his signal to have sex after dinner. That meant he would be okay this evening. She went to the bedroom to shower. She took her twenty dollars out of the sock she'd been wearing, placed it in a clean sock, and shoved it in the back of her top drawer.

"Ow, that hurt," she said to herself as she lifted her shirt over her head. She caught a glimpse of her bruises on the bathroom mirror. The bruises covered her back, her shoulder, and her arm. She turned the water on in the shower, entered it, and cried.

9

Stan About Dorika

Lynn was into her usual routine, up early and dressed for work. She and Alan had a quiet late evening, with mostly surface chatting. He was still asleep as she left for the hospital.

"Good morning, all," Lynn said, starting the meeting with her management team. "Let's begin with a report from the Social Services department. Terry, go ahead."

"Last month, Suzanne and I saw one hundred and ten patients. Sixty-eight percent of them involved domestic violence, twelve percent end-of-life issues, sixteen percent financial issues, a mixture of caring for a now disabled family member, managing autistic children, and working with children services. More specific disease issues impeded their lives, like not climbing stairs and driving a car. We did identify two trafficked victims, too," reported Terry.

"Are you satisfied with the way we are structured to handle the domestic violence situations?" asked Lynn.

"We do fine with the kids as far as the system goes. The nurses do a phenomenal job of case findings. Our biggest issue is working with adult women who do not want us to report they are being abused to the police or the state agency. Without their consent, we cannot do anything about intimate partner violence. If they are severely injured, a family member can take over with power of attorney and say yes to reporting them," said Terry.

"That's great. I have a meeting with a detective today about abused adult women. The police are consulting with a psychologist about talking with abused women and developing a safety plan. I'll find out more about how we can get involved," Lynn responded.

The meeting went on with reports from other areas of the department. After the session ended, Lynn checked the hospital database to see when and if Dorika had ever been seen in the ED.

She searched for Dorika Boglarka. Her last name was given to her by the office at the assisted living facility. The screen lit up, describing four visits to the ED in the past two years. She wrote down the days and injuries.

January 2018: Wrist sprain—upper arm bruising noted

July 2018: Dislocated elbow—upper arm bruising noted—long sleeve top on ninety-two-degree day

February 2019: Severe abdominal pain with bruising

November 2019: Fractured jaw with a black eye

Lynn was going to show this to Stan without Dorika's name on it, of course. Her sense was Dorika is being abused for sure, and the beatings are escalating to more severe injuries. She grabbed her coat, purse, and information and left the hospital.

Lynn looked out over the Cape Fear River before she entered the restaurant. Something about the river and the ocean on the east side of the city relaxed her. Stan waved to her from his table near the window.

"Hi," he said. "Good to see you." He bent his six-foot-four-inch frame over to hug her.

"Same here," Lynn responded. "How are you doing?"

"Great. Carol's off at college, coming home soon for the holidays. Eddie is a junior in high school. They still miss their mom, who you know died four years ago but doing okay. When my kids are good, I'm good," said Stan.

The waitress was at their table. "I'll have a fish sandwich with a wedge and some hot tea," said Lynn. "I'll take the check, too."

"Your lobster roll for me and coffee, thanks," replied Stan. He started to protest Lynn picking up the check, but she gave him that look that he knew met arguing was futile.

"So, what can I help you with this cold winter day?" asked Stan. "Don't even hesitate to call me, by the way. Our meetings are so much better than most of the rest of my activities."

Lynn explained her encounter with Dorika, without mentioning her name, and described her trips to the ED.

"So, you are handing out your mom's twenty-dollar bills. What a great idea she had there. Glad to see you are following that tradition," replied Stan.

"Really? You have lots of dealings with people whose financial lives are pretty marginal. Do you think that's okay to do?" asked Lynn.

"Are you kidding me? Of course. If more people helped impoverished people out, there would be fewer crimes. I always saw a policeman's job as trying to put ourselves out of business. Twenty dollars is not a lot of money, but it's a lift. It's a sign someone cares about them, too. At least that's my view, for what it is worth," said Stan.

"As you mentioned on the phone, you want to know how to help this woman get out of an abusive relationship. Right? What she's experienced qualifies as a *pattern of abusive behavior,* the state guidelines for domestic violence. In North Carolina, she could petition the courts for a restraining order against her husband and get him thrown out of their house. There are also women's shelters if she's afraid he'll come after her even with a restraining order. It is less complicated because they don't have children. I think the broken jaw could land him in jail. The law is supportive of her, but she has to admit he abused her and is okay reporting it to authorities," explained Stan.

"She wouldn't admit to me she was abused, but those finger marks and bruises on her arms tell me a different story. She also winced a little when I hugged her," said Lynn.

"Trust your instincts on that. They are good ones. As I mentioned, we have this psychologist consulting with us. I brought some information on him and a copy of the handouts from his talks. He says, don't push it. Act like you care and like them without judging. We know sometimes they are embarrassed and believe it is their fault they are getting beat up. Be sympathetic, saying stuff like, 'Sorry this is happening to you - it's not your fault.' Tell them help is available without trying to talk them into it."

"I get it. We push to rescue abused women. I ...

All of a sudden, a different waitress was at the table. It took a minute, but Lynn recognized Theresa from the toy store.

"I had to come over to thank you again. What you did was another sign we did the right thing moving here. Christmas will be happier because of you and your mom," said Theresa.

"You are more than welcome, Theresa. Have a wonderful holiday!" Lynn said.

"A happy recipient of the twenty-dollar bill?" asked Stan.

Lynn nodded, yes.

"Policemen don't see many good deeds. We understand the sad and often painful underbelly of lives. So sitting here, seeing this woman come up to you happy because of your kindness, I, too, feel joy. As I said, it is a great thing your mom started."

Lynn touched Stan's arm. "Thanks for that."

"Keep in touch. I like our luncheons," said Stan as they got up to leave. "I'm happy to do as many as you need."

"Since you like our luncheons, what would you think about having lunch or dinner with Mom and me at her apartment at the assisted living complex?" asked Lynn.

"Besides the company of two wonderful women, I might, by chance, meet your friend in need?" replied Stan.

"That's why you are such a good detective—you figure plots out quickly," said Lynn.

10

Lynn and Alan

LYNN WALKED INTO THE APARTMENT TO THE AROMA OF clams' linguini. Alan did not cook often, but this was one dish he excelled at making. It was one of Lynn's favorite meals, too.

"What's the occasion?" asked Lynn, eying the dozen red roses on the table. "Yum, linguini with clams," she said, kissing Alan on the cheek.

"Do you remember last month? I got an offer on a three-million-dollar house on the beach?"

"The one on Ocean Point Drive in Wilmington?"

"Yep. We closed today. In this sale, I was both the listing and selling agent—one-hundred-eighty-thousand-dollar commission, which I split between the company and me. Finally, I have financial success."

"Congratulations. That's great news. I'm happy for you."

"No, sweetie, it is good news for both of us. We can get married and buy a great house. What do you think?"

"This is wonderful news, but a surprise," said Lynn. Wow, thought Lynn, what's happening here?

"I know I act like a prick sometimes. I'm sorry about that. I know I get carried away with stuff like the wine and the way you dress."

"The way I dress?" asked Lynn. "I don't remember you saying anything about the way I dress."

"I didn't want to say much. You don't pick out the most flattering clothing. Who wears jeans and loose tops, anyway? That's pretty juvenile for someone your age."

"I'm thirty-four—not exactly ready for vintage wear."

"I just think you should wear more sophisticated clothes. I'm happy to go shopping with you and help you pick out clothes," said Alan.

"You don't like me doing charity work, you don't like my jewelry preferences, and now I've learned you don't like the way I dress. Why do you want to marry me and buy a house together?"

"You are an asset to me. When we go out together, especially to functions with potential clients, you are wonderfully friendly and beautiful. Everyone likes you. You help me get clients."

"I guess my real question is, why should I marry you and buy a house together? I'm a commodity to you—not a love partner. I also don't particularly like being judged by you all the time. You act like you are the supreme court of wine pairing, dressing, and jewelry wearing."

"I thought you liked our lifestyle. I didn't know you took my comments personally. It's just my way to make you a better person."

"Alan, you don't get it. You think you are so superior to me. If I married you, I'd have a life of someone correcting me all the time. Plus, you like it that I support you and your goals, but what about my dreams? What kind of support do you give me for a life that's meaningful to me?

"Here I thought we were doing great. What changed?" asked Alan.

"I guess it is other people in my life who treat me with kindness and respect. They support me, not tear me down as you do."

"I don't know what to say. I don't understand why you are unhappy. I was just trying to be helpful."

"Really? You think continually criticizing someone is helpful?" asked Lynn.

"I didn't know I was critical. I just thought I was putting you on a better path than you are on," said a confused Alan.

"What makes you think your path is better than mine? I give up. Please sleep in the guest room tonight. We can pick this up tomorrow," said Lynn.

11

Work and Theresa

The next morning Lynn was up and dressed and out the door before Alan woke up. Thank goodness for work, Lynn thought, driving to work. Is this the end of Alan and me? Is there any hope for us? At least I did what my mother suggested. I told him how I felt. Three ambulances were in front of her ER as she arrived at work. Thoughts of Alan would be on the back burner.

"What's happening, Suzanne?" said Lynn to the nurse manager, Suzanne, in charge.

"There was a trailer truck and a three-car pileup on the highway earlier. A car tried to pass an eighteen-wheeler in a no-passing zone from what the police can piece together. That car was on track for a head-on collision with an oncoming vehicle. The truck driver started blasting his horn and pulled over into the shoulder to give the cars extra room. The passing car hit the side of the truck, forcing it into a ditch. As he continued trying to pass the eighteen-wheeler, the driver ended up hitting the car coming toward it."

"Wow, what kind of injuries are we seeing?" asked Lynn.

The truck driver, Daniel Johnston, has a badly bruised shoulder but nothing broken. He's getting x-rays done to make sure nothing is fractured. The fellow driving the passing car, Harry Conway, is unconscious with a head injury. He's going up to the neuro ICU about now. The couple in the oncoming car, Mr. and Mrs. Reynolds and their five-year-old son, Christopher, were hurt. The driver's side of the car got smashed in. Mr. Reynolds, the driver, has fractured ribs, a left-arm fracture, and a leg fracture. His wife has a wrist fracture. Christopher has some bruises but no sign of fractures. He got scared and is still talking about being in the car and hearing the crash. It looks like the people in the car that went into the pileup, Mr. Thompson and his twenty-four-year-old son, Richard, just got bruised. They are down at x-ray right now."

"Sound like it could have been worse, with a truck and three cars," commented Lynn.

"The truck driver was a real hero in this scene. Honking his horn and pulling over helped diminish the impact of the accident, the police said. He also called nine-one-one as soon as he saw what was going to happen. Ambulances and fire trucks got to the scene quickly." Suzanne took a deep breath.

"Also, he went to check on the people in the cars. Somehow, he jacked up the part of the vehicle crushing the driver of the oncoming vehicle, Mr. Reynolds. He was having trouble breathing from the pressure. I don't know much more about that, but it seems the truck driver probably saved his life."

"And how are you all doing, Suzanne? What can I do to help?" asked Lynn.

"I'm fine. If you could talk with the families in the waiting area, that would be a big help. We are so busy with the patients right now."

"You got it. I'll check on each patient and then see the families. I'll check in with Beatrice first since she's in charge. Do you know where she is?" asked Lynn.

"Where who is?" asked Beatrice heading down the hallway toward Lynn.

"Hi, Beatrice, how's it going? Is Mr. Conway set to go to the neuro ICU?"

"We are taking him right now. I talked with the family, and they are going to meet us upstairs."

"How's he doing?"

"Not great. Conway's vital signs are stable, but he's in a deep coma. The docs are worried he might have permanent brain damage. They are going to do some more tests after a few days as long as his signs don't change," replied Beatrice.

"Any issues with anyone because he caused the accident and all the injuries?" asked Lynn.

"Nothing that affected his care. It's always hard when the perpetrator of a crime causes injuries and is in the ED at the same time as the victims. The sympathy always goes to the victims. We did put Mr. Conway's family inside the nurses' lounge to separate them from the families of those that got hurt."

"Good planning. You all are doing such a great job. Thank you for that. I'll check on the rest of the patients and go talk with the family members," said Lynn. "I'll go check in with Bruce first.

"Hi, Bruce. How are Mr. and Mrs. Reynolds and little Christopher? I understand you are taking care of all of them," asked Lynn.

"Mrs. Reynolds is doing well. She has a cast on her wrist and will need PT once we remove it, but it was not a bad fracture. She and Christopher are in the same room. Mr. Reynolds is another story. His femur is fractured and needs surgery. His radius is fractured and is already in a cast. He has rib fractures, but none are dislocated. He'll be okay but with a long recovery."

"Thanks for all your excellent care, Bruce. I know they are were in good hands," said Lynn, feeling proud of her staff.

The Thompsons weren't back from the x-ray department yet. Lynn went out to the waiting room.

She found the Reynolds family first.

"How's my mother and father?" asked Julia Reynolds. Lynn guessed her to be around twelve years old. She was there with an older woman who might have been her grandmother.

"Your mom and dad are doing fine. Your mom has a cast put on her wrist and should be able to go home soon. Christopher is with her. He has a bump on his head but nothing serious. Thank goodness for seat belts and booster seats. Your dad is getting ready to go to the operating room to get his leg fixed. You can go in to see him before he goes up to surgery," explained Lynn.

"I'm his mother. I want to see him, too," said the senior Mrs. Reynolds.

"But of course," said Lynn. She took them back to Mr. Reynold's room.

Lynn went back to the waiting area to see the relatives of Daniel Johnston, the truck driver. A distressed woman came through the door, frantically looking around.

"Theresa," Lynn called to her. "Can I help you?"

"Lynn, what are you doing here? I heard my husband was in an accident. No one would tell me anything over the phone," said Theresa, anxious and stressed.

"First of all, your husband is fine. He has a sprained shoulder. He's getting an x-ray right now to make sure there are no fractures. Come with me over here. I have some more to tell you," said Lynn.

"Okay," Theresa said. Her hands were still shaking.

Lynn explained her role at the hospital and what they knew about how the accident happened.

"In addition to what I just told you, the police are saying your husband is a hero. His actions helped avoid a worse accident, and he probably saved the life of one of the victims by lifting the part of the car that fell on him. The police will know more when there's a complete investigation of the scene," explained Lynn.

"What? Daniel is a hero?" asked Theresa.

"Sure looks like it. It's a good guy you have there, Theresa. He should tell his boss a raise is in order. He saved the truck, too. Come on. I'll take you back to his room where you can see him when he comes back from x-ray." Lynn guided Theresa to her husband's room.

At the end of the day, as Lynn drove home to get ready for dinner with Peter, she wondered about bumping into Theresa again. She wondered if having more contact with twenty-dollar recipients happened to her mother.

12

Dinner with Peter

LYNN WAS HOME ALONE, GETTING READY FOR HER DINNER with Dr. Peter Fry. Even though they had done lunch and dinner together several times, Lynn felt a little nervous about tonight. She had already tried on three different outfits and was working on a fourth.

This is ridiculous, she thought. *It's just dinner with Peter, a friend, a single friend*, she added. *I'm going with the blue cashmere v-neck sweater, navy Ponte knit pants, and red heels. Casual but a little sexy*, she thought.

Peter was at the restaurant when Lynn arrived. He had already ordered a margarita for both of them—hers with no salt. He always remembered how she took her coffee and her margaritas.

"Hi, Peter," she said as she sat down.

"Hi, yourself," Peter said. He held up his glass to toast with her. "Good to see you outside of work."

"What a day. This dinner out is precisely what I needed," said Lynn.

"I think my entire orthopedic staff spent their day in the ER and OR. Keeps the juices going." Peter said, sitting back on the cushioned booth.

"Did the ED staff do what you needed them to do?" asked Lynn. She knew he would say yes, but if he told her that, she could go back to the staff and give them his feedback.

"It was smooth all morning. Patients were monitored well, back and forth to x-ray in good order. Then up to the OR or an inpatient bed or, better yet, out the door, in record time. You have a well-oiled machine system in that ED." Peter smiled broadly at Lynn.

"Your orthopedic group treats them well, too. No big egos or narcissists like some other surgeons we won't mention." Peter and Lynn both laughed, knowing quite well about the misbehaviors of Dr. Donald Simmons. Lynn threatened to take him to the hospital board after throwing a roll of bandaging tape at one of her nurses. She, fortunately, ducked in time to avoid getting hit. The chief of surgery suspended him for a week after that incident.

Lynn and Peter reviewed the menu.

"I'll have the fish tacos with the guacamole appetizer," said Lynn to the waiter.

"Beef enchiladas for me with a cup of chicken tortilla soup," requested Peter.

"Shall we get business out of the way while waiting for dinner?" asked Peter. "Keep drinking your margarita, though."

"It's never a good sign when you want me to get drunk before asking for the supplies you wish to have."

"You know me too well," laughed Peter.

"So, what do you need?"

"We want to switch over to double-sided felt roll splints. We have found them to be easier to use. They also prevent moisture exposure with fewer skin macerations. We've tried a few that we purchased ourselves with success. But we need them stocked in the ED, so they are easily accessible."

"Sounds easy enough. Is it okay with the powers that be in the hospital?" asked Lynn.

"Yep, all approved. The residents and docs all prefer to use them. They sent letters of recommendation to the CFO. It's just a question of who will pay and stock them. They come in four sizes, by the way."

"Whose budget are you thinking about?" asked Lynn.

Peter held his head down and whispered, "The ED's."

Peter looked so sheepish; Lynn couldn't help but laugh.

"Okay, so how much money are you looking for?" asked Lynn

"Here are the figures. We looked at how many patients in the last six months came into the ED where we could have used these splints. We see about one thousand orthopedic patients a month in the ED. Of those, we could fit about two hundred and fifty patients with splints. We need an initial stock of these splints for about ten thousand dollars, and replacements we figure will cost maybe four thousand dollars a month. Winter months might be higher because of slips and falls. Summer months might require more splints because of craziness at the beach!" explained Peter.

Lynn knew it was the upfront stocking fee that's the significant financial issue. She also knew her budget could easily manage these splints. Insurances would cover most of the cost as the braces get used, too. But maybe she would tease Peter a little.

"Wow, ten K. That's a big ask. Any perks for the staff?" asked Lynn.

"New coffee machine? Flowers? Candy? Continuing ed talks?" offered Peter.

"Now, you are just joking around. You already do all that for the staff," replied Lynn. "Okay, we'll cover the stocking fees and then hopefully will recoup when the insurance companies pay for the splints that are used. I need to run this by the CFO, but I don't think it will be a problem. He always figures out how to break even or even make a little extra money for our budget."

"Okay, that concludes the business part of our dinner. Now we can talk about other stuff? How's everything going with you, Lynn? How's your mom?" asked Peter.

"Just a minute! One more piece of business. Whose department is paying for this dinner?" asked Lynn with a slight smile.

"Well, my dear, since you have been so gracious, it will come out of the orthopedic budget." Peter brought up his glass and toasted with Lynn again. "To business dinners with a beautiful colleague," he said.

There was a look between them for a few seconds. *Peter's such a good guy*, thought Lynn.

Their dinners arrived. Lynn went on to chat about her mother and George and his family. Lynn laughed as Peter talked about how his eight-year-old daughter, Hanna, wants a hammer and saw for Christmas, like her dad. They ended dinner, agreeing to have more of them before Christmas.

13

Dorika

DORIKA CAME HOME FROM WORK, EXHAUSTED. AMBRUS WAS not back yet. She took a shower and climbed into bed for a quick nap. An hour later, Ambrus came home.

"What the hell are you doing?" yelled Ambrus. He grabbed her by the arm and jerked her out of bed.

"I come home after working all day at that crappy restaurant instead of being the teacher I once was to find my wife in bed. I have to listen to women complain; they don't like this, they don't like that, about the food. I use to be respected—now I'm a garbage receptacle for food complaints from the ignorant. Go make me dinner," Ambrus shouted. He pushed Dorika toward the kitchen, causing her to slam into the doorframe.

"What's the matter with you? Can't you walk straight?" Ambrus grabbed her, pushing her again toward the kitchen.

Dorika was on the floor. Blood was dripping from above her left eye.

"Stop it," she said.

"And who is going to make me?" yelled Ambrus heading toward Dorika.

"I am." Dorika stood defiantly in the kitchen with a knife in hand.

"Okay, enough," said Ambrus. "I'm going to shower. Supper better be on the table when I get out."

Dorika nodded in agreement.

What was I thinking? She said to herself. *It will be worse when Ambrus gets out of the shower.*

She checked the shower, but Ambrus was not in it. Dorika went to the bedroom to grab her prepacked bag and her sock, where she hid her money.

"So, you think you can make me stop doing anything I want to you," he said, coming up behind her. "Well, you can't." Ambrus grabbed her by her arm to turn her around toward him.

Dorika felt something wet and warm on her hand. Ambrus let go of the hold he had on her. She ran to the bathroom and locked the door.

"Come out of there, you bitch. I'll get you for this," yelled Ambrus, banging on the door.

Dorika could hear Ambrus kicking at the bathroom door. She jumped when she heard a hard push against the door, probably by Ambrus's shoulder. She quickly put the small bathroom chair against the doorknob.

She opened the bathroom window. "Help, help. My husband is trying to kill me. Call the police. I need help," she cried over and over again.

What did I do to provoke Ambrus? Why didn't I just keep quiet, Dorika thought. She was now cowering in the corner.

There were sounds of knocking and the doorbell ringing at the outside door to the apartment. "What's going on in there? We can't have all this yelling and screaming here. The police are coming. Answer the door," the voice of Randy Sheeran, the superintendent of the building, said. "I want to make sure everyone is all right."

Dorika listened carefully. Ambrus was no longer yelling or kicking against the door. *Should I go out,* she wondered. *Maybe he is there waiting for me.* She could only hear the voice of the superintendent and the sirens. She waited.

"Dorika, are you all right?" said Randy Sheeran, the superintendent, sounding closer, maybe right outside the bathroom door.

"I'm in the bathroom," she replied. "Where is Ambrus?"

"He's not here; it's just me and the police. It's safe to unlock the door," said Randy.

"How do I know Ambrus is not making you say that?" asked Dorika.

"Miss, I'm Officer McDonald with the Deer Park Police Department. It's safe now. Mr. Boglarka is not here."

Dorika got up from the floor and slowly walked to the door. Her face and back hurt. A quick reflection in the mirror showed blood dripping down her face. She unlocked the door. A look of horror came over Randy's face.

"Let me help you," Randy said. He held her arm at first and then put his arm around her back for more support.

"Miss, can you tell me what happened here today?" Officer McDonald asked once Dorika was seated on the living room couch.

"My husband dragged me out of bed and slammed me into the doorframe. Then he threw me on the kitchen floor, where I hit the edge of the counter. He came after me again, and I picked up a knife to protect myself." Those few sentences took all the energy Dorika had for the moment.

"He backed off and said he was going to take a shower. He left the kitchen, so I ran to get my stuff and leave, but he wasn't in the shower. He tried to grab me again, but I ran to the bathroom." Exhausted, she stopped.

"I've seen the black eyes and other bruises," said Randy. "He's a monster. How about we let the EMTs look at her?"

"Good idea," said McDonald.

The EMTs patched up the cut over her eye.

Dorika heard one of them say, "I think she might have fractures on her face and maybe ribs. She needs to go to the hospital for x-rays."

In the ambulance, Dorika replayed the scene in her apartment. She remembered the warm, wet feeling coming from Ambrus when he turned her toward him. *Did I stab Ambrus*, she wondered. *Did he go down the back stairway? Could he have done that if I stabbed him?*

14

Stan, Dorika, and Dorothy

It was six-thirty p.m. when Lynn arrived at her mother's apartment building.

"Hi," she said to Stan when he arrived.

"What's in the bag?" Stan asked. "Was I supposed to bring something?"

"Just Chinese takeout. Mom figured it was better to bring food in rather than having the kitchen staff deliver food, leaving them wondering why Dorika was here."

"Smart. Does Dorika know I'm coming?" asked Stan.

"That she does, and she's looking forward to talking with you. Dorika and Ambrus had a big argument that turned more violent than usual. That's all I know," said Lynn.

"Hi, Mom," Lynn said, hugging her mom. "Hi, Dorika. Good to see you." Even though the bruises on her face had faded and had make-up covering them, Lynn could still detect their presence. "Dorika, this is Stan Gregowski. Stan, Dorika."

Stan shook Dorika's hand. He couldn't help but notice how thin her arm was and how frail she looked overall.

"Hi, Mrs. Price. How are you? So good to see you," said Stan.

"Please call me, Dorothy. Happy to have you here." Dorothy always liked Stan and his family. He was a good kid growing up and always delivered their paper on time.

"Let's eat. I'm starving," Lynn said, spreading the various containers of Chinese food on the table. She had also made hot tea for everyone.

"Wine, anyone?" Lynn asked. Everyone said yes. Lynn set wine glasses and a bottle of pinot grigio and merlot on the table.

Toward the end of the meal, Lynn asked, "Dorika, how are you doing? Mom said you had a tough week, but I didn't get any details."

"Ambrus hit me a lot. I think you noticed that, Miss Lynn." Lynn nodded, yes.

"On Wednesday, I came home tired and took a nap. Ambrus comes into the bedroom, drags me out of bed, and throws me against the bedroom door frame. He comes again and throws me onto the floor in the kitchen. I got up and grabbed a knife from the counter. 'No more,' I said. He said okay and that he would take a shower. I went to the bedroom to get my bag of stuff and my sock with my money in it when I noticed Ambrus is not in the shower. He grabbed me from the back and turned me around. I got free and ran to the bathroom, locked the door, and yelled out the window. The building superintendent and police came. Ambrus was gone."

"I'm so sorry you have gone through all this. Did you go to the hospital?" asked Lynn.

"Yes. The ambulance took me. The doctors put stitches on my face and did x-rays. The doctor said the x-rays showed bones in my arms and legs were broken a long time ago," responded Dorika.

"So where are you now, Dorika, with all this? Where are you staying? Did you get your things out of the apartment?" asked Lynn.

"I don't know what to do now. Maybe you can help me. When I went to the hospital, I took a bag I had packed before and my purse. I still have some clothes and other things in the apartment. I'm afraid to go back in case Ambrus is there," said Dorika, obviously frightened.

"Where are you staying now?" Lynn asked again.

"Miss Dorothy said I could stay here for a while until I find a place to stay," Dorika answered.

Lynn looked at her mother and shook her head but smiled. It was not a surprise her mother would do that. Fortunately, the security in the building was excellent.

"Let's see if we can ask the superintendent of your building to change the locks on your apartment. In the meantime, I can get a police officer to go with you to your place to collect your things. Do you know whose name is on the apartment lease?" asked Stan.

"No, I don't know. Maybe both me and Ambrus. I know I signed something because I had a full-time job."

"Good, I'll call the superintendent and find out," said Stan.

"I can go with Dorika to her apartment," suggested Lynn.

"No, that's too dangerous. I've dealt with people like Ambrus, and they don't give up easily," Stan warned.

"There's something else," Dorika said. "The police said they found my blood and Ambrus's blood in the apartment. It looked like Ambrus was bleeding a lot. This part, I don't remember well. After Ambrus said he would take a shower but didn't and then grabbed me from behind, blood dripped from him. I don't know if I still had the knife or if Ambrus had the knife. I don't remember if I took the knife with me from the kitchen."

"Did you have the knife with you in the bathroom?" asked Stan.

"No, I know I didn't have it there," said Dorika.

"So one of two things could have happened. If you had the knife when Ambrus grabbed you from behind, you could have stabbed him when he turned you around. If he held the knife, he could have maneuvered you, so you hit his arm holding the blade, and it went into him. The pathologist might be able to help us out with that. We also use a hypnotherapist who might be able to help you remember exactly what happened," said Stan.

Dorika nodded in agreement.

"Do you know where Ambrus would go?" Stan asked Dorika.

"Maybe with his cousin, Tadeo. He does not live too far," said Dorika.

"Write down his address, please," Stan said, handing her his notebook with a page open. Dorika's hand shook as she wrote.

"This could get tricky. If I were you, I'd file for a restraining order against Ambrus. He could say you attacked him and tried to kill him. You have a record of being injured, and he does not, does he?" asked Stan.

"Ambrus never gets hurt. He protects himself," replied Dorika with anger in her voice.

"Here's something you can do to start getting ready for the legal processes. Take a picture of any bruises you have now. Write a record of times you have been physically, or psychologically or sexually abused. If he calls or texts you, record the phone calls and texts. If you have friends and neighbors who know about instances, such as you running to their house for protection, get them to write down all those events. Sound okay?" asked Stan.

Dorika nodded, yes.

"Let me turn off the GPS on your cell phone, so Ambrus can't track you. Who pays for your phone service? If he does, he can check your phone calls if he knows your password," suggested Stan.

"My phone is through here, this senior center. They had a good deal but only for me," said Dorika.

"So, let's recap here," said Lynn. "I'll work with you, Dorika, to get the restraining order. Stan is going to get a police officer to go with you to your apartment. He's going to talk with the superintendent about the lease. Maybe also see if the super is willing to change the locks on the entrance door to the building and the flat. Do we need to put her in a more secure place? This building is pretty safe but not designed to keep out abusers."

"Let me see if we can either move her to a securer place or station an officer to watch the building," said Stan. "I'm assuming the office here doesn't know Dorika is staying here, right?"

Dorothy nodded. "No one knows, as far as we know. Dorika is on sick leave for this week."

Stan left both Dorothy and Dorika one of his cards. "Call me any time. Ambrus is dangerous. Keep Dorika out of sight for now."

"Thanks, Stan," Lynn said.

Stan and Lynn left together on the elevator. "This is worse than I had expected. Sorry to drag you into this, except you were so helpful," said Lynn.

"You and your mom were the best neighbors growing up. When my wife got sick and died, you were there for me. I'm happy to help out." Stan took Lynn's hand and squeezed it gently right before the elevator door opened.

15

Alan

Lynn went home feeling drained. Alan wasn't back yet. She poured herself a glass of merlot and turned on the TV. *I need to unwind for a few minutes*, she thought to herself and promptly fell asleep until Alan came home.

"Hi, honey, I'm home." Alan was in the hallway, taking off his coat. "Hope you had a good day because I had a fabulous one."

"Tell me about your fabulous day," Lynn replied. *It's like nothing ever happened as far as Alan is concerned,* thought Lynn.

"I got a contract on a two-million-dollar house this afternoon. It's gorgeous. I wish we could afford it," replied Alan.

"That's great—good for you."

"I thought we could celebrate and go out to dinner tonight," said Alan. "You pick the place since you have such good taste in restaurants."

"Sure, sounds good. Give me a few minutes to think about where to go and check who has availability tonight," Lynn replied. *Hmm, he paid me a compliment. He always thinks he's better at picking restaurants. Maybe something sunk in,* thought Lynn.

"Deer Park Seafood Company has an opening at eight o'clock. We can make that," suggested Lynn.

"I don't know. That last meal I had there wasn't great. Anything else available?"

I don't remember going there with Alan. I wonder with whom he went there. Expensive and romantic for a business dinner, mused Lynn.

Lynn checked some more restaurants. "How about the Boathouse? You liked their flounder the last time we were there."

"I don't know about that one. What else you got?"

"Since this is your celebration, Alan, why don't you pick the restaurant?" *Throw in a new girlfriend while you are at it, too*, thought a frustrated Lynn. *He is not going to change. I need to either accept him as he is or get out.*

They arrived at the Lighthouse Inn around eight. Soft music played in the background as they were escorted to a lovely table/booth combination with no one too close.

"May I bring you a beverage to start your meal?" the waiter asked.

"I'm looking over your champagne selection. What is your best-selling brand?"

"Our Moët & Chandon brand is excellent and well received."

"You have a few choices under that name—which do your customers like the best?" asked Alan.

"Like all wine, it depends a lot on your palate. I have the impression you have a sophisticated one," said the waiter. "The two most popular champagnes are the Nectar Impérial and the Moët Impérial. The Nectar Impérial has a peach fragrance with a hint of white flowers and clover combined with a delicate palate of core fruits. The Moët Impérial embodies Moët & Chandon's unique style distinguished by its bright fruitiness and sophisticated maturity."

"Lynn, what do you think?" Alan asked.

He knows I don't care that much for champagne. Maybe the fruitier one would be best for me, she thought.

"I think the Nectar Impérial," she responded.

"Bring a glass of the Nectar Impérial for my lovely lady and a glass of the Moët Impérial for me," said Alan.

"I'm sorry, sir, but these champagnes can only be ordered by the bottle."

"Lynn, since I know you won't drink that much champagne, how about we get the bottle of Moët Impérial for the table? Is that okay with you?"

"Sure," said Lynn.

"So how was your day, Lynn?" asked Alan.

"I'm not sure you would be that interested in my day," she responded.

"Sure, I am. Whatever happens to you is important to me."

"Today was about the same in the ED. It was busy with this flu going around but manageable. Yesterday was interesting, too."

"Tell me," said Alan.

"The woman I gave the most recent twenty-dollar bill is getting beat up by her husband. Most recently, he slammed her against the door frame and bruised her up pretty badly. The police were called, but her husband had fled the scene. I talked with her and a detective that helps us with abuse cases in the ED. The detective and I went over how to keep her safe and get her ready for court."

Alan looked at Lynn, not knowing what to say. Then it hit Lynn. *Wow*, she thought, *I have been missing the bigger picture of this relationship. He has no interest in what my life involves at all.*

16

Lynn and Alan

"Hey, Sis," said George on the phone. "You got some time to meet with Angie and me about Christmas?"

"Sure, when is a good time for you guys?" replied Lynn.

"How about Sunday for dinner?" said George.

"Sure, that works for me. Sounds like fun. What can I bring?" responded Lynn.

"You up to bringing one of your key lime pies with the strawberry sauce? Please!"

"For you, bro, and your family, I'll do it. See you around six o'clock?"

"Sounds good. Just don't forget the pie," said George.

Lynn laughed and hung up.

Lynn got home before Alan. It was her night to make dinner, and she started on a meatloaf dinner.

"Hi, Sweetie, I'm home. Yum, meatloaf, my favorite." He came over and kissed Lynn on the cheek.

"How was your day, Lynn?" Alan asked. Lynn recognized now that Alan did not want to know about her day. She decided to give him the gory details anyway.

"It was good. A man came in with a fishhook in an eye, another man had a fractured femur from falling off a roof, and a teenager came in having an asthma attack. The rest were not as critical, such as someone with chest pain that turned out to be a panic attack. There were some patients with minor cuts that needed stitching. So busy, but not crazy. How did your day go?" asked Lynn.

"Showed a few houses but no new contracts. I have a closing tomorrow, which should go well. Nothing as exciting as your day," said Alan. "I don't know how you do it."

"You know I love my job and love helping people," Lynn replied.

They were having their after-dinner tea when Lynn started her awkward conversation.

"Alan, I was thinking about us," she said.

"We are doing so much better, don't you think?"

"In fact, no, I don't think we are doing better. I think we are pretending a lot," replied Lynn.

"I don't get what you mean."

"It dawned on me the other day. I know there are a lot of women who would love the life you want. You want to be rich and live a sophisticated lifestyle. Would you agree?" asked Lynn.

"Yes, of course. I want financial security. I want to be able to buy a fifty-dollar bottle of wine without thinking twice about it. I want my wife to buy elegant clothes and jewelry. I want a nice house that I'm proud of."

"Exactly," said Lynn. "But that's not what I want. I want to help people and make a difference with my life. I want a nice house and nice clothes but not any showplace—just something comfortable. I want a place where my family and friends could visit and feel relaxed."

"I don't get what you are saying. Does that mean you don't like the jewelry I bought you?" asked Alan.

Oh, this is going to be more challenging than I anticipated, thought Lynn.

"It's not about the jewelry, or the clothes or the house. It's about what we both want out of life," said Lynn. "It's about who we are as individuals."

"I don't know where you are going with this. It's making me nervous," responded Alan.

"Alan, for months now, I have been angry with you about criticizing me about handing out the twenty-dollar bills, buying me jewelry I don't want, plus other stuff. Finally, I realized something. There is nothing wrong with what you want and like, and there is nothing wrong with what I like and want. The problem with us is we want different things that don't mesh well together."

"But we get along so well. I love taking you to my events. Everyone says how beautiful and smart you are. You are a wonderful asset to my work," countered Alan.

"Thank you, Alan, but I want someone who admires me not because I help them get ahead and make more money. I want someone who admires me because I sat with the man with the fishhook in his eye to keep him calm until he went to surgery. I want someone who thinks it's great. I honor my mother by handing out twenty dollars to someone who could use a little boost. You don't think that's great."

"You know, I think those people should get a job and not expect handouts," said Alan.

"Yes, Alan, I do know you think that. That is your right. But being caring and charitable is meaningful to me, which you don't understand."

"You are right about that. I don't understand. So, what's your point?" said Alan.

"We are just making each other unhappy by not approving what we each value," said Lynn. "There are lots of lovely, intelligent women who would love to share a life with you the way you want that life to be. I'm just not one of them." Lynn hoped that would get through to Alan.

"Are you breaking up with me?" asked Alan.

"Yes, and I'm trying to free us both up to find someone who would be happy with what we each want from life and how we want to live that life. I do not fit in your framework of life, and you don't fit in mine. We are just hurting each other, trying to convince the other person to change."

"I think this is just more of your psychological babble," replied Alan. "I think we are great together. I love you even though I do not always agree with what you do. All couples have issues. You are making a big deal out of nothing like you always do."

17

George and Angie

It was Sunday, and Alan had left to show a house to a client. He was in a great mood, believing this was the perfect house for this wealthy client and his family.

"Have a good time at your brother's," he said to Lynn as he kissed her on the cheek goodbye.

"Good luck with this house," replied Lynn.

This is insanity, thought Lynn. *I never thought it would be so hard to break up with someone.* She mulled over her talk with Alan while driving to George and Angie's house.

"Hi, sis. So good to see you," said George. Angie came over to hug Lynn.

"It's good to be here," said Lynn.

"Oh, oh. I detect a note of relief to be out of the house," said George. "Is Mr. Sophistication getting to you?"

"If you want to hear about it, I'll give you an earful," replied Lynn.

"Great," said Angie. "If you want to say hi to the kids first, they are in the bonus room. Then we can talk. Last I saw of them; they were in an intense game of Go Fish. Bernie has them now playing with two decks. They have already eaten so that we can talk over dinner."

"Here's your merlot," George said.

After Lynn said hi to Bernie, Edison, and Eloise, they sat down to a dinner of barbeque chicken with mashed potatoes, asparagus, and a side salad.

"This dinner is delicious," said Lynn. "Thanks for having me over."

"Never mind the small talk. Spill about Alan and you," said George.

"I came to see that Alan and I just are not compatible. There are plenty of women who would love to live the life Alan wants to set up. I'm just not one of them. I told him that, but he didn't get it."

"So besides being a pompous ass, he's also a knucklehead. Right?" said George.

"George!" admonished Angie. "Let her talk."

"I think George is right, although maybe not the name-calling so much. Alan tells me he loves me and criticizes me at the same time. He wants me to be someone different than who I am. I think who I am is okay."

"You know George, and I think you are a terrific person. I could not have asked for a better sister-in-law," said Angie. "So, where did you leave it with Alan?"

"I want to get out of this relationship, amicably. Alan doesn't hear that that is what I am saying."

"Hurray!" said George loudly. "This is a wonderful day. When are you moving out?"

"George!" said Angie.

George's hurray was so loud, Bernie, Eddison, and Eloise came out to see what was happening. "Did someone win the lottery?" asked Bernie.

"Dad is just exuberant," said Angie. "No one won anything."

After a little eye-rolling on Eloise's part, the three went back to their game.

"So, Lynn, what are your plans?" asked Angie.

"I don't know what to do at this point. I don't want to invest more time into this relationship with Alan. Honestly, I'm tired of him always correcting me. I tried to present the breakup to not hurt anyone, but that didn't work. Suggestions?"

"Just move out," said George. "Talking is not working. Whose name is on the lease? When do you renew it?"

"We both signed the lease," Lynn said. "It's up the middle of January. I don't think Alan renewed it. He keeps talking about buying a house."

"Find another place and move out," said George. "Simple."

"Do you think counseling would help?" asked Angie.

"I don't know. The last time we talked, Alan accused me of talking psychological babble."

"It would tarnish Mr. Perfect's reputation, too. He wouldn't do it," said George.

"Would it help you, Lynn?" asked Angie.

"I don't know. I'm mad enough at him for always being critical of me to want to get out. He's ready to take the next step in the relationship—get married and buy a house. I don't want to do that with him."

"That's settled. You just need to find a place and move out. DO NOT tell Alan you are moving out. That can be dangerous," warned George.

"What about furniture, et cetera? Do you have much of your stuff in the apartment?" asked Angie.

"Joint checking accounts?" asked George.

"Fortunately, our finances are separate, although Alan does know the password to my accounts. I'll check them. The dining room table, chairs, and the hutch belong to me, along with my bed and dresser. The rest of the furniture belongs to Alan. This is so overwhelming," Said Lynn, with tears in her eyes.

"We'll help you," said Angie and George in unison.

"You know you can stay with us as long as long as you need to," said George. Angie nodded in agreement.

"That's nice of you guys. Thanks a lot. I don't know what I would do without you," said Lynn giving both Angie and George a hug.

18

Dorika and Randy

DORIKA WENT BACK TO HER APARTMENT, ACCOMPANIED BY A policeman, to get some clothes and her toiletries. Her key no longer worked in the lock. *Ambrus changed the locks,* she thought. *Maybe the superintendent will let me in to get my stuff.*

"Randy," said Dorika, knocking on the superintendent's door. "It's Dorika from upstairs."

"Hi, good to see you. How are you?" Randy asked, nodding to the policeman.

"I am okay these days. But I came to get some stuff from my apartment, and my key doesn't work. Did Ambrus change the locks?"

"Not Ambrus. I changed the locks so he couldn't get in. A detective named Stan Gregowski called to check on the lease and the locks on the door. I told him I'd change them. I also took Ambrus's name off the lease."

"You can do that?" asked Lynn.

"A clause in the lease states anyone who commits a violent act on the premises, are removed from the premises and the lease. So only you are allowed into that apartment."

Dorika started to cry.

"Don't cry. Everything will be okay. Come in, and I'll make you some coffee or tea," said Randy.

"I'll wait in the hallway," said the police officer.

"Thank you so much. You are so kind," replied Dorika. She sat on the edge of the couch in Randy's living room. She had been here before when she and Ambrus signed the lease.

"Tea or coffee?" asked Randy.

"You don't need to bother," said Dorika, "but tea would be nice."

"No bother," said Randy. He went into the kitchen to make the tea.

Dorika blotted her eyes and took some deep breaths. She tried to relax and let go of all the tension.

Randy came back with the cup of tea on a tray next to milk, sugar, and some chocolate chip cookies.

Dorika smiled.

"Nice to see you smile," said Randy.

"Thank you for your kindness."

"I'm also going to change the lock on the front entrance. I was waiting until you came back. I hope you will stay in the apartment again if it's not too uncomfortable. Mrs. Sullivan moved out of her apartment. It's smaller than yours, but the rent's a little cheaper, too. I can move you into that one," Randy said hopefully.

"On my goodness, that would be wonderful. This apartment is so convenient to work. People are nice here, including you," said Dorika.

"Great. I'll draw up another lease. I'll transfer the security deposit from your current apartment to Two-C, Mrs. Sullivan's old place. The new apartment's security deposit is a little less, so you will get some money back. Also, to attract new renters, we just started offering the first month free to those who move in. Since you will be in a new apartment, I can include you. You'll be paid up until February 15 since you are paid up until January 15 now."

"You are so kind," said Dorika. "How can I ever thank you?"

"Your safety is thanks enough. I always thought Ambrus abused you, but you never complained. So, I did nothing. Now that you are speaking up, I can do something to help. No one should abuse you like that."

Dorika suspected Randy had seen abuse before. She thought some other time she would ask about it.

"Thank you for the tea. Can we go to my apartment now and also check out Mrs. Sullivan's living quarters?

"Of course," said Randy.

The three of them went upstairs to Donika's old apartment. The police officer went in first to check if the apartment was safe. There was no sign of Ambrus.

Lynn called Stan Gregowski as soon as she heard about the accommodations the superintendent was making.

"I'm assuming you'll believe the new apartment and lock changes will make it safe for Dorika to live there," said Lynn.

"I agree it is safer, but also, I know she won't have to worry about Ambrus anymore," said Stan. "I had put a BOLO out on Ambrus. He was in your hospital, Lynn. He died in the OR a few hours ago. We are waiting for the autopsy results. If his death is from the knife wound, Dorika might have some more troubles," said Stan.

"Oh, no, that poor woman. When you come to talk to the pathologist, let me know. I'll treat you to lunch," said Lynn.

"It's a date," said Stan right before he hung up.

Lynn called Dorika. There was no answer. She left a message that she would see her at Dorothy's apartment around six p.m. Then she called her mother.

"Hello," answered Dorothy. "How are you, Lynn?"

"I'm fine, Mother. Always good to hear your voice. Have you talked with Dorika today?"

"Yes, I did. Dorika is so excited about what her superintendent is doing for her. Are you worried it still won't be safe?" asked Dorothy.

"No, she will be safe there. She might have another worry. Ambrus is dead, Mother. He died in my hospital today in the OR. We are waiting for the autopsy report. She might have another worry if he died from a stab wound," explained Lynn.

"Oh, no. Dorika can't seem to get a break," said Dorothy.

"I told her I'd meet her at your apartment today at six. I hope that was okay?" asked Lynn.

"But of course, it was okay. I'll have dinner sent up for us. See you then."

Lynn finished up her office work and took a quick tour of the ED. There was a patient with chest pain, a teenager with a sprained ankle, a woman who had overdosed with sleeping pills, and a man with a dog bite. A physician had seen all the patients. There were ready to be sent home or transferred to a unit upstairs.

Lynn was off to see an apartment and a house closer to both work and where her mother lived. A new phase of her life was beginning, thought Lynn.

19

Lynn and Alan

LYNN DROVE OUT OF THE HOSPITAL DOWN TOWARD HOPEVILLE Beach. Her thoughts were swarming.

It feels so good to relax a little and head toward the beach, she thought. *Being closer to the water will be a good move.*

"Hi, Lynn," said Angela Thompkins. "Good to see you again. It's been a while."

"I guess so. I do not even remember the last time I saw you. Maybe at the holiday party downtown for the Marshalls," said Lynn.

"Is this apartment or house for you and Alan? "Angela asked.

"No. It's just for me. I would so appreciate you keeping that under your hat. I don't want the rumors flying. Please also don't say anything to Alan about where I'm looking to live."

"Okay. That was loud and clear. The information is in my vault!" replied Angela. "Let's look at the apartment first, and then there's a house I think you might like. I know you have an appointment at six o'clock, so we'll be quick. Viewing these places will help me figure out what will work for you."

"Sounds good," said Lynn.

"This is the building I told you about. There's a three-bedroom apartment up on the twelfth floor," said Angela.

"Wow," said Lynn. The apartment was empty. However, as Lynn walked in, she saw the fantastic view of the ocean from the sliding windows. She walked over to the window, opening it up to a fifteen-foot balcony.

"Can you walk to the beach?" Lynn asked.

"It's a little over a mile away. There is a parking lot near the water that the tenants can use. Let's look at the rest of the apartment."

"Are these terrazzo countertops?" asked Lynn.

"Let me check the specs. Yep, good eye! Check out the pantry. It's huge."

The three bedrooms were down the hall with the two smaller rooms on the right with a full bath in between. The master bedroom was on the left with the same ocean view as the living room minus the sliding doors. It had a large walk-in closet with a separate tub and shower.

"Nice apartment, Angela. How much is it?"

She checked her papers. "It's nineteen hundred and ninety-five dollars a month plus another hundred for parking in the parking area under the building."

"It's beautiful but a little pricey," said Lynn as they left the apartment building.

"Let's go to the next stop. We will see a three-bedroom house in the Dune Plantation section. It is a sprawling ranch with a two-car garage, about nine years old," Angela said.

On arrival, Lynn said, "I like the landscaping. Magnolia trees are my favorite."

"This is lovely," said Lynn walking into the house. She quickly moved from the entranceway through the kitchen, dining room, and three bedrooms. Lynn was checking off the list of requirements in her head—kitchen with granite countertops, pantry, window, separate dining area, master bedroom with a walk-in closet, full shower, wood floors, a two-car garage. It had everything she wanted plus an extra half bath. "Two and a half baths are nice," said Lynn.

"This one is two hundred and ninety-five thousand dollars. I think the owners are anxious to sell. Maybe the price can come down a little. With a typical mortgage of twenty percent down, you are talking about a fifteen hundred dollar a month mortgage, including taxes and insurance. I'm afraid you still need to drive to the beach—about two miles away, but this house is not in a flood zone."

"I like it," said Lynn. "Let me talk with my brother and have him look at it, too. Thanks, Angela. I'll be in touch."

She drove over to her mother's apartment and noticed it was only a ten-minute drive from the house. She wasn't looking forward to telling Dorika her problems weren't over yet.

When Lynn arrived, she saw the food service had just delivered dinner. Dorika was in the back room, out of sight of the delivery staff.

"It's okay to come out, Dorika," said Dorothy. "The delivery girl has left, and Lynn is here."

"Hi, Dorika. Good to see you again," said Lynn.

"You two talk. I'll get dinner on the table," said Dorothy.

Lynn and Dorika sat on the couch. "I have some news for you," said Lynn. She took Dorika's hand. "Ambrus is dead. He had come to the hospital because of his wound and died during the operation. He'll never hurt you again."

"Oh, no," said Dorika, shaking a little. "How can that be? He was always so strong."

"They are doing an autopsy. We should know soon," replied Lynn.

Tears were running down Dorika's face. Lynn couldn't tell if they were tears of sorrow or relief or maybe even both.

"Sorry to bring this up, but you need to know this. Depending on the autopsy report, if the cause of death is a knife wound, you might be investigated. It might mean going to court. There's plenty of evidence Ambrus abused you. The police and EMTs saw the bruises, plus the records of your abuse are at the hospital. If he died because of something else, you wouldn't need to go to court; I don't think," said Lynn.

Dorika was now crying loudly and hard. Lynn held her to her.

"It never ends," Dorika said through the tears.

Lynn drove home exhausted. Alan's car was in the garage. She hoped the evening was going to be pleasant.

"It's about time you got home. Where were you all evening?" Alan asked.

Lynn thought she would tell him she was out to dinner with this gorgeous doctor but refrained.

"I was having dinner with my mother," Lynn replied. "Why?"

"If you remember, we were supposed to go to the country club dinner tonight. I tried calling you, but you didn't answer. What's going on with you?"

Lynn so desperately wanted to tell Alan she was moving out but remembered George's warning about not saying anything until she had moved out.

"Sorry, I forgot about dinner. I'm tired. It was a busy day at work, and my mother wasn't feeling well. I thought you had an evening house showing," replied Lynn.

"I did have an evening showing, but I canceled it at the last minute. I, fortunately, remembered this country club dinner in time for me to go. I thought you were keeping track of our social engagements. You must keep your phone on all the time for situations like this. You embarrassed me by not being there tonight. Don't do that again."

Lynn still had her keys in her hand and her purse on her arm. She turned around, walked out the door, and headed to her brother's house.

20

Dr. Peter and Moving Out

THERE WAS A KNOCK ON LYNN'S OFFICE DOOR. "GOOD MORNing, my dear. How are you today?" said Dr. Peter Fry. He plunked himself down in the cushioned chair in front of Lynn's desk. Even sitting down, Peter looked like he was moving. His tall, lean frame matched up with his exuberance reminded Lynn of basketball players. Like them, he was at maximum readiness for what was going to happen next.

"I am particularly good today. Thank you for asking." Lynn smiled back at Peter.

"Okay, spill. Something good has happened. Come on—let it out," smiled Peter.

"You promise you won't breathe a word of this to anyone?" requested Lynn.

Peter did a pretend zipper movement across his mouth. "It will go immediately into my vault. Most of the time, I don't even remember what is in that vault or where it is."

Lynn laughed. "Okay, I am moving out of the apartment I share with Alan and am buying a house. Meanwhile, I'm staying with my brother and his family. That's quite fun!"

"Wow! So, you finally left that pretentious SOB! Good for you. I think a dinner celebration is in order. What evening works for you?" Peter had taken out his phone and opened it to his calendar. "What are you doing on Saturday night?

Lynn looked at her desk calendar. "Lo and behold, I am free on Saturday. Sounds wonderful."

"I'll pick you up at seven o'clock at your brother's?" Lynn nodded, yes. "It's a date," said Peter winking at her.

So, how does Peter know where my brother lives? thought Lynn. *How does he know Alan is pretentious? Hmm.*

Lynn left work a little early to meet up with her brother at her apartment. She planned to get all her things. She had left Alan a message but got no response back.

She was relieved George was coming with her. He had arranged for the security guard at the apartment building to be with them if there was trouble.

I'll be so glad when this is over, thought Lynn. Her heart was racing. *May there be no conflicts.*

Lynn, George, and the security guard took the elevator up to Lynn and Alan's apartment. Lynn opened the door to the apartment and immediately heard Alan's voice and that of a woman. They found Alan and a woman sitting at the kitchen table with papers and pictures of houses scattered about. Lynn recognized the woman, Francine, as another realtor in Alan's firm.

"Hi," said Alan. He got up from the table, kissed Lynn on the check, shook George's hand, and nodded to the security guard. "Francine and I were just going over some houses that are for sale. I want a place with a superb view of the beach with four bedrooms and three baths. Want to see some pictures? There's an amazing pocket listing that Francine says she can get me a good price. Plus, since I'll be representing myself, I save three percent of the commission."

"Good for you, Alan. I think I'm just going to go pack up some of my clothes. I'll make arrangements to have movers take bigger stuff," replied Lynn.

"Take whatever you need. When I get this new house, I'm buying all new furniture. What we have here has served its purpose, but I want to go more upscale," countered Alan.

"Thanks, Alan. Sounds great." Lynn left to go to the bedroom to start packing what she needed immediately.

The security guard sensing the situation was amicable and not violent, shook George's hand. "I'll be going back downstairs. You know how to reach me," he said.

"Thanks, Tom. Much appreciated," replied George.

"Hey, Alan. I'd like to look at your pictures. Angie and I are thinking of moving, too. You got anything in the one and a half to two million dollar range near the beach, Francine?" asked George, laud enough for Lynn to hear.

It took all her composure to stifle a laugh when she heard George talk about the more than a million-dollar house. She knew George and Angie had no interest in moving. She also knew George had read Alan's motives for having Francine here. He was his pretentious self, trying to make her regret not marrying him and not moving into this gorgeous house he was planning to buy. George had just one-upped him as only George can do, knowing Alan couldn't afford a home over a million dollars. She was sad, though, that Alan had no idea that a fancy place was not a motivator for her after all their time together.

Armed with four suitcases, two stacked on two others, Lynn entered the kitchen area.

"Good luck with the house hunting," she said to Alan and Francine. "I'll be in touch to move out the other stuff of mine, Alan. Take care."

"I know what you were doing," Lynn said to George in the elevator. "I know you and Angie have no plans to move."

"You never know what we might do in the future. Maybe Alan and I will be neighbors," said George.

"You know he couldn't afford anything over five hundred thousand dollars."

"Yep!" said George. "Just wanted to knock him off his ostentatious pedestal."

Lynn gave him a soft sock to his arm.

"I'm telling Mom you hit me again."

They both exited the elevator laughing.

21

Stan and Dorika

"WE GOT THE CORONER'S REPORT ON AMBRUS THIS MORN-
ing. It's a little iffy as to the cause of death," said Stan on the phone
with Lynn. "I remember you saying I get lunch with you when this
report comes in. Is today a good day?"

"Today is an excellent day. We could have lunch here in the hospital, but maybe something more private would be better. How about
the Chinese restaurant on Fifth Street? *Gourmet Chinese*. That's usually
rather good," said Lynn

"How about one-thirty? The lunch crowd should have thinned out
by then," replied Stan.

"Perfect. I'll meet you there," said Lynn.

If the staff took care of Ambrus in the ED, Lynn knew she could
get a copy of the coroner's report. Otherwise, she had to wait until she
met with Stan. *I think I'll wait until I meet with Stan. Poking around
where I'm not authorized is not a good idea,* she thought.

"Hi, Stan. Good to see you," said Lynn. She hugged him and sat
across from him in a booth at the end of a long string of tables. Stan

must have *strange information to choose to be this sequestered,* Lynn thought.

Lynn ordered her usual cup of wonton soup and shrimp dump-lings. Stan also ordered wonton soup but with a dish of shrimp with lobster sauce.

"I'm dying to hear. What did the coroner say?" asked Lynn.

"First of all, Ambus did have a knife wound in his abdomen. It was a one-inch deep wound with a wide cut surface that the coroner thought was due to someone twisting the knife. If it had been cared for properly, the cut would not have killed him. Some antiseptic wash, Steri-strips, and a clean gauze cover would have been adequate, although the ED staff would have stitched him up if he had gone there. But he came in with an infected wound caused by no cleaning and, according to the staff, 'a dirty rag' over the wound. The docs had put him on antibiotics, but he was getting worse, almost septic, with a high fever. The surgeons took him to surgery to remove the infected tissue and some of the surrounding tissue. He went into cardiac arrest on the table.

"Wow! That's a terrible set of events. What was the official cause of death?" asked Lynn.

"The cause of death was the infection. The problem is the chain of events leading to death was the knife wound. The knife had both Ambrus's and Dorika's fingerprints on it. That doesn't tell us much. They both lived in the apartment and could have used the knife at any time," said Stan.

"So, it is still important that we know who stabbed Ambrus. Right?" asked Lynn.

"Yep. That's a big part of the case if it's filed against Dorika. She still was being physically abused, with a lot of proof of that. However, there's a new wrinkle," added Stan. "Ambrus had a stash of money in the apartment and a bank account to the tune of four hundred and fifty thousand dollars or thereabouts."

"Wow! Does anyone know where he got so much money? That gives Dorika motive, right?" suggested Lynn.

"Sure. Ambrus was beating her and hiding money. If she knew about the money, killing him would stop the abuse and make her well off, at least for a while," replied Stan.

"Dorika mentioned once that Ambrus was a teacher in Hungary. I checked teacher salaries at the time. They made about seven thousand dollars a year, with living costs being cheaper there. One of the reasons he wanted to come to the US was to make more money. When he got here, he had to go through a teacher preparation program, certification in specific subject areas, and demonstrate proficiency in reading and writing in English. I don't know if he tried any of that. He eventually got a job as a waiter. I'm not sure where, but Dorika would know. He could have been doing something on the side to make money. I know he took all of Dorika's paychecks, but she's lucky if she gets paid minimum wage. She's had a sad life," commented Lynn.

"Makes you grateful for the problems we have, doesn't it? Dorika also says she doesn't remember what happened with the knife she had in her hand in the kitchen after Ambrus left. Right now, her testimony doesn't help her at all, although I haven't heard anything about proof she knew about the money," said Stan.

"You had mentioned at one time to have her undergo hypnosis to gain some memory of the event. Do you think that's still worth doing?" asked Lynn.

"North Carolina, like other states, has gone back and forth about the admissibility of hypnotized testimony in court. There are a few forensic hypnotherapists in this state that work with the police. These hypnotherapists insist on having the session videotaped so the jury can see there were no suggestions offered to say one thing over another. The DA might look at hypnotized testimony before going to court. I don't know where the case is with the DA, but I can find out through the detective who has this case," replied Stan.

"Wow, this is messy. Let's do that and see where the DA is with the case. If the DA doesn't want to file charges because of the abuse history, Dorika is home free. Does the money piece make that less likely?" asked Lynn.

"If there's a way to prove Dorika did not know about the money, that would help. It's very tough to prove someone doesn't know something, although not impossible. For example, Ambrus could have bragged about having that much money while saying Dorika knew nothing about it."

"If he did, I'll bet it was to his cousin. Dorika alluded to them being competitive," replied Lynn.

Lynn paid the bill.

"Thanks for lunch," Stan said as they headed for the door.

"Thanks, Stan, for helping with this. It means a lot," said Lynn.

"You have helped other officers and me with many the cases that came through the ED. It's the least I could do. Plus, you know you are my favorite nurse!" Stan said, smiling broadly.

"I also know you say that to all the nurses," responded Lynn.

"Nope, just to you," replied Stan. He bent over and hugged Lynn, then headed toward his car.

22

Work and George

Lynn was at work Saturday morning. It had been a busy Friday night with many patients for her to check on. "Hi, Mrs. Rodriguez. Your son, Berto, is ready to be transferred up to pediatrics. His asthma is much better, but the doctor wants to watch him overnight. There is a cot available for you to sleep in his room if you wish."

"Thank you, thank you. That will calm me. You are so kind," said Mrs. Rodriguez.

"You are more than welcome. I'll call the unit to have a cot ready for you for tonight. Just call me if you need anything."

Lynn went over to speak with the policeman in charge of a car accident investigation.

"Hi, Tom, how's it going for you?" asked Lynn

"It's a mess," said Detective Tom Berringer. "We are still sorting out who did what to whom and under what circumstances. We are waiting for definitive alcohol levels on everyone. It does look like the four college kids in one of the cars were drinking. There were bottles of beer in their car. The two men in the other cars had just left a bar before the accident. We think the truck driver fell asleep. No evidence that he was drinking."

Lynn looked at her sheet of patient names and their injuries and dispositions.

"We have two of the victims in surgery—the college student who was in the front passenger seat and one of the men. We think the man in surgery was the driver of that car. The truck driver has some bruises and abrasions but mostly from the airbag as far as we know yet. They are still doing tests. The rest of the patients are either being patched up or going for more tests. It's going to be a while before we get them all physically assessed and treated."

"We are here talking to them and your staff when we can. We just don't want anyone leaving the ED until we say it's okay for them to leave," replied Tom.

"I hear you. All the staff working right now know the drill. Just come over to my office or text me if you need my help with anything. You need my number?" asked Lynn.

"Thanks, but I have permanently listed your number on my phone's speed dial," said Tom with a small laugh.

Lynn worked on the staff scheduling and inventory of supplies. Because it was Saturday, there were fewer interruptions from the administration and other department heads. She liked her Saturday schedule.

"Now, to go home and get ready for dinner with Peter," she mused.

"So, are you getting ready for your big date tonight?" teased George when Lynn got home. "I was trying to remember the mean things I did to your dates when we were kids. There had to be some dramatic scare events."

"Let me see. Harry Gagnon got buzzed by some electronic fixture when he rang the doorbell," said Lynn.

"Oh, yes, my electronic age," laughed George.

"You mortified poor Jonathan Clark when you invited him to sit in the chair in the living room on top of the hidden whoopie cushion," said Lynn, shaking her index finger at him. "Tell me you haven't planned anything juvenile like that for Peter."

"Oh, no, I'm way beyond the juvenile stuff. You'll see," said George. He did his monster laugh.

"George, stop teasing your sister. You are a knockout in that blue dress, Lynn. Love the heels," said Angie.

The doorbell rang. To Lynn's great relief, there were no screams of distress from Peter.

23

Dinner with Dr. Pete

GEORGE ANSWERED THE DOOR. "HI, DR. PETE. SO GOOD TO see you."

"Hi George, how have you been?" Peter shook George's hand.

"I've been good. You know, though, we have a questionnaire for you to fill out before you can take Lynn out."

"George!!" yelled Lynn and Angie at the same time.

"What? I'm just looking out for my little sister. I remember this guy from high school and college. We can't be too careful," responded George.

George and Peter did this weird hand ritual for the benefit of Lynn and Angie.

"So that's how you two know each other. I wondered how Peter knew where you lived when he said he'd pick me up here." Lynn also wondered if there had been more communication about her between them. She put that on her to-do list to find out.

Peter turned to Lynn, smiling. "Are you ready, my dear?" he said. "While parting is, you know, sorrow, the restaurant awaits us." His left elbow was bent toward her waiting for her arm to enter. The two walked out the door with their heads held high as if walking down a promenade. Lynn managed a behind-her-back goodbye wave to George and Angie with her free hand.

As she entered Peter's car, she realized they had never driven together. She had always taken her car to wherever they were meeting. *I had not thought about the feeling of closeness being in a car together brings up,* Lynn thought. *Scary.*

After they were seated, Lynn looked out the window from the *Dockside Grill* restaurant to the inlet. There was a small island there, which was the summer home of goats and peacocks. She loved watching them roam the island together in the warmer weather. *Who would think about putting peacocks and goats together for customers to watch,* thought Lynn?

"We will have to come here in the summer to see the goats and peacocks," said Peter.

"So, you know about them?" said Lynn. "This is my favorite restaurant. How did you happen to pick this one?"

"Oh, it's my favorite, too." Peter smiled. "Plus, George told me how much you like coming here."

"Hmm. So, what else has George been telling you?" asked Lynn.

"First of all, George knew I always had a crush on you. George disliked Alan with a vengeance. He figured if he kept telling you what a pompous ass Alan was, someday I might have an opportunity to pursue a relationship with you beyond work." Peter poured more merlot into Lynn's glass.

"So, my brother has gone from playing tricks on my dates to matchmaking. I have to say matchmaking is a much better hobby. Tell me about this crush you had. Did I meet you before we started working together at the hospital?" asked Lynn.

"Yep! When George and I were in college, I came over to your house to pick him up for a get-together with friends. That's when I saw George's gorgeous sister, who was a senior in high school. It was instant infatuation!"

"I'm sorry I don't remember meeting you," said Lynn.

"George said you had a pretty nice boyfriend already. Life just went on from college to med school."

"My boyfriend Henry was the only one George never harassed. The rest of them became one-date wonders out of fear for their lives," laughed Lynn.

Peter laughed in acknowledgment of George's reputation for antics. "He always was a creative fellow."

"If you don't mind me asking, I know you got married and have a daughter. What happened there?" asked Lynn.

"Virginia and I met while I was in med school. She was an interior designer working at my mother's house. She introduced me to art and designs, which fascinated me. We dated and then got married. It was good at first, but the glue wasn't there. Hanna, my daughter, was a godsend for a while, giving us a common emotional bond. It wasn't enough, though. I became over-invested in work, and Virginia became over-invested in someone else. We got divorced amicably and now share custody of Hanna, who just turned eight."

"How about you?" asked Peter. "George only describes your past loves in general terms like, 'nice guy but the IQ of a turnip,' 'his feet don't touch the ground,' and, of course, 'pompous ass' as you've heard."

"Yes, I have heard them all. My history contains Henry, the boyfriend in high school. He didn't go to college, but I did. That created a big divide. I dated a business major in college for a few years. He wanted to get married, but I didn't feel strong enough about him. I worked as a nurse in the ED in Charlotte, North Carolina, when I decided to go back to school to get my master's degree. Once I finished that, I came back to Deer Park and got the job as ED director. I met Alan through a friend, and we dated for a few years, and then moved in together. Now I'm moving out."

"I love the timing for us," laughed Peter. "Let's toast to getting to know each other even better."

Lynn toasted happily but became nervous, too. Deciding to walk away from Alan had been exhausting. She wasn't ready to get too involved with someone else, yet.

24

Dorika

"CAN I MEET WITH YOU AND DORIKA TO GIVE YOU AN UP-date? It's mostly good news," asked Stan. Lynn was at work but was anxious to hear what Stan had to say.

"Sure. Tonight, at Dorika's new place? Same building, but apartment number Two-C."

"See you at seven o'clock?" asked Stan.

"We'll have pizza ready," replied Lynn.

"Great, see you then," said Stan.

Lynn called Dorika to make sure she was available.

"Of course. I can't wait to hear the news," said Dorika. "My new apartment is a mess; otherwise, I'd cook something."

"I'll bring pizza and a salad and maybe a dessert. Don't worry."

Lynn arrived a little before seven.

"Hi, Dorika. You have a great view of the river in this apartment," said Lynn.

"Randy has been so great. I feel very safe," answered Dorika.

The doorbell rang, and Dorika let Stan into the apartment.

"Hi, Lynn. Good to see you both," said Stan.

"Let's sit and eat and talk. Does that work for you two?" asked Lynn.

Dorika poured each of them a glass of red wine and laid out the pizza and salad Lynn had brought.

"This is Bull's Blood wine," said Dorika. "Don't worry; it doesn't have bull's blood in it. The name is from a story about the Turkish invasion of Eger. Supporters gave the Hungarian troops this wine to drink, which was said to have bull's blood in it to give the soldiers strength. During the battle with the Turks, the Hungarians won the battle even though their army was smaller. This wine is drunk a lot when people need strength."

"What a great story and a great idea to serve it," said Lynn. "Now that we have strength, Stan, what news do you have?"

"The detective in charge of the case talked with the DA. With all the abuse history in Dorika's case, the DA said, even if she did stab Ambrus, she doubted any jury would convict her. She's not going to bring her up on charges."

"Wow, that's great news," said Lynn.

"There's more good news. Since the DA is not going to press charges, Dorika can pick up all of Ambrus's possessions and what the police found in the apartment. That includes the fifty thousand dollars they found hidden in their living quarters and the additional four hundred thousand dollars in his bank account.

"Oh, my God," said Dorika. "That's a lot of money."

"Don't thank me just yet. There's a small caveat. As his wife, Dorika is entitled to all the money Ambrus had and all the apartment possessions. There is a small possibility another relative, like his cousin, could contest this case. He could say she killed him and doesn't deserve to receive the money. Chances are if someone contests the case, it will go to civil court. There would be no risk of going to prison, but if Dorika lost, she would have to give up the money."

"Yikes," said Lynn. "Any suggestions for what she should do?"

"I think she should hire a lawyer to keep on retainer. Right now, the court will release anything that is in Ambrus's name to Dorika. A lawyer can handle all that," said Stan.

"Dorika, do you have anything that has both your names on it?" asked Lynn.

"I have some money that I hid from Ambrus, at about four hundred dollars. It was all the tips I made. I wanted to escape, but I needed money to do that," explained Dorika.

Lynn thought about the twenty dollars she had given Dorika. How many more women are there who need escape money?

"There is something else that could help along with hypnosis. It's called crime scene simulation. Say Dorika gets hypnotized. She remembers what happens with the knife. If Dorika stabbed him in the simulation, the simulation shows what the knife wound would look like. If Ambrus held the knife when he pulled Dorika toward him and got stabbed, the simulation would show what that wound would be like. Then it's back to the coroner to examine the wound again," explained Stan.

"Wow, that sounds like a great idea," said Lynn.

"What do you think, Dorika?" asked Stan.

"Do you have the name of a good lawyer? And yes to the hypnosis and this crime scene simulation," said Dorika.

"Here are the names of three lawyers. Feel free to tell them I recommended them to you. Talk to them about this idea. Here's the name of the forensic hypnotherapist I have recommended in the past. She's particularly good and has credibility with the police."

Lynn hugged Dorika right before she and Stan left. "It will all work out for you, Dorika," she said.

"It's better already. I'm not getting beat up anymore," said Dorika.

Lynn and Stan left for their cars. "I can't even imagine living the way Dorika did. I just left Alan because he was so condescending and demeaning. So many women live with much worse," Lynn said to Stan.

"You left Alan? Are you OK?" asked Stan.

"I'm still adjusting and staying with George and his family in the meantime. It's hard at times, but it was the right thing for me to do," replied Lynn.

"Let me know if there's anything I can do for you. Would dinner out help?"

25

George and the New House

"ARE YOU READY," ASKED GEORGE. "YOU DON'T NEED TO BE all gussied up to see Angela and the house you are thinking of buying."

"I wasn't gussying up," said Lynn. "I just wanted to look nice after working all day."

"Okay," said George.

"Do you need directions to the house?" asked Lynn.

"Nope, I'm good," replied George.

"Thanks for doing this, George, and for going over the finance piece."

"Of course. You are my baby sister, plus it's what I do in business."

As they drove up the driveway of the house, Lynn smiled. The house felt perfect to her.

"Hi, Angela," said Lynn. "This is my brother, George."

"Good to meet you. Come on in," said Angela. "Let's do the tour for your brother, shall we?"

"It's a two-car garage," Angela said. George pushed the garage door opener. He put the bottom of the broom he found in the garage under where the garage would close and pushed the button again. The garage door stopped before hitting the brush. "Good," said George. "No water or mice droppings, either."

As they went through the house, George flushed all the toilets, ran all the water faucets, climbed up to the attic, and generally snooped. Angela and Lynn chatted, sitting at the kitchen table until he finished. Lynn told Angela she totally liked the house and would get back to her the next day.

"Let's take a ride through the neighborhood," George suggested. "Check out the types of cars in front of the houses. It's a good way to determine the character of the neighborhood."

"Lots of SUVs—Toyotas, Subaru's, Hondas, Chevys, and Nissans. The sedans are mostly Camrys, a few Lexuses, Infinitis, and Mercedes. An occasional truck, but not many. How's that sound?" asked Lynn.

"Sounds great," said George. "That's a typical middle- to upper-middle-class neighborhood car display."

"Thanks for all your checking in the house. Did you find anything?" asked Lynn.

"A few little things. For example, one of the sinks doesn't drain as fast as it should, but that's not a big problem. The inspector will find anything else that needs fixing. It's not that old to have a lot of questionable aspects," said George.

"Let's swing by the beach," suggested Lynn.

They went back to the house and calculated the distance to the beach. It was 2.4 miles.

"That's good. It puts you out of the flood zone," said George. "Are you going to make an offer? I'd support that. You need some money for the down payment?"

Lynn laughed. "Aren't you the wonderful brother?" She reached over and kissed George on the cheek. "I have enough money saved up for the down payment, but thanks."

"I use Barclay Trust downtown. I'll call John Harrison and let him know you are coming to see him. Ask for him when you call to set up an appointment. What are you think of offering?" asked George.

"As I remember what you told me about this type of deal, two hundred and eighty-five thousand dollars would be reasonable. The owners could come back to two hundred and ninety thousand dollars. Given the comps in the neighborhood, that would be acceptable to the banks. If I put twenty percent down, say sixty thousand dollars, or maybe seventy-five thousand dollars. I could get a two hundred and fifteen-thousand-dollar mortgage easily with my salary. Make sense?"

"Where did you learn all that? You must have a great brother who taught you all that," teased George.

Lynn punched him gently on his arm.

"I'm driving," said George indignantly. "I'm calling Mom to tell her you hit me and almost caused me to have an accident."

"Hello, George," says Dorothy on the phone.

"Mom, Lynn hit me again. She ..."

"You probably deserved it. Lynn only does that when you are not behaving. Behave yourself," replied Dorothy doing everything she could to stifle a laugh. Click went the phone.

Lynn and George both laughed gleefully like the children they once were.

26

Dorika

"Good morning, Angela. I've decided to put an offer on the house. What's the next step?" asked Lynn.

"That's great news. I'll send a contract to your email. You will need to include what you want to pay for the house. We will need an earnest money deposit of a thousand dollars to hold the house. That gets put into an escrow account with us. If you close on the house, we will fold that thousand into your closing costs," said Angela.

"Suppose the deal doesn't go through? What happens to that money?" asked Lynn.

"Our contracts say the money will be returned to you if you cannot get financing, if the house doesn't pass the home inspection, or if the home doesn't get appraised at the asking price. If you just change your mind, the money goes to the seller," clarified Angela.

"Fair enough. Send over the contract, and I'll fill it out. I can drop it off at your office with the earnest money check. How's that sound?" asked Lynn.

"Sounds good to me!" said Angela.

Okay, that's off my to-do list, thought Lynn. *What else is going on today?* She thought as she checked her schedule. *I need to take Dorika to the hypnotherapist this morning—that should be interesting.*

"Good morning, Dorika. How are you this morning?" asked Lynn.

"A little nervous. Never have been hypnotized before," responded Dorika.

"What makes you nervous?" asked Lynn.

"They can make you do funny things you don't want to do," said Dorika.

"You mean like cluck like a chicken?" Lynn checked if that idea was on Dorika's mind.

Dorika nodded her head, yes.

"Hypnosis cannot make you do anything you don't want to do. Stage hypnotists ask people to do strange things for entertainment. Hypnosis with a professional is more like therapy. Serious stuff," said Lynn. "Remember, you can leave any time, too."

"Okay," said Dorika.

"Good afternoon," said Dr. Susan Kemper to Dorika and Lynn. "We are all ready for you."

Dr. Kemper directed Dorika to the reclining lounge chair.

"As I said over the phone, this session will be videotaped in case you need it for court. In most states, like North Carolina, information obtained under hypnosis can be used if it helps the defendant. They like to see the video of that session, so the court knows you have not been prompted by the hypnotherapist to say something specific, explained Dr. Kemper. "Do you have any questions, Dorika?"

"I am nervous. What if I say the wrong thing?" Dorika asked.

"There is no right or wrong thing. You just describe what happened to you as you remember it. Under hypnosis, you can remember things you can't remember ordinarily. Do you remember who your teacher was in the third grade?" asked Dr. Kemper.

"I don't think so. That was a long time ago," said Dorika, trying to remember the third grade.

"That memory, though, is stored in your memory bank. You could recall it under hypnosis," said Dr. Kemper.

"I see," said Dorika. "What happened with the knife with Ambrus is stored, too, right?"

"Yes. We are going to release that memory today. Are you okay with that?" Dr. Kemper knew sometimes people were coerced into getting hypnotized. She doubted that was the case with Dorika but has learned to always check.

"Yes. I'm nervous, but I want to do this," said Dorika.

"Good. I'd like to do some pretesting with you before we start. If you would stand up for a moment and close your eyes, put both your arms out with the palm up on your right hand and thumb up on your left hand. I want you to use your wonderful imagination and imagine I had placed a large book on your right hand. Maybe you see the book, or perhaps you do not. Maybe it is a book you own. You can feel the weight of the text on your right hand. Your right hand is slowly going down, down, down from the heaviness of the book. Maybe you feel an ache in your muscles.

On your left thumb, imagine I have tied a string that's attached to a huge orange balloon filled with helium. Your left hand is going up, up, up as the balloon pulls it up to the sky. The right hand goes down, down, down as the book's weight gets heavier and heavier. The left hand goes up, up, and up as the balloon pulls it up.

Don't move your arms, but open your eyes," Dr. Kemper requested.

"My right arm is down below my waist, and my left arm is higher above my waist. What does that mean?" asked Dorika.

"It means you are open to following suggestions in hypnosis. You will do well in the session. I have a few questions for you. What did you see?" asked Dr. Kemper.

"I could see a big orange balloon. I could feel the book but not sure what it was," explained Dorika.

"How's your right arm?" asked Dr. Kemper.

"It's a little sore from holding up the book. Wait a minute; there was no book. How come it hurts a little?" asked Dorika.

"Great questions. Your arm will feel fine in a minute. Those reactions show me you are visual and kinesthetic, meaning you take in information by what you see and feel. That's good for me to know when I am hypnotizing you. I will use words like see and feel, for example, in the session," Dr. Kemper explained.

Dr. Kemper started on the video camera, attached Dorika to the GSR machine, and turned on soft, comforting delta wave music.

27

The Hypnosis Session

"Dorika, close your eyes and let yourself sink deep into your chair. You will soon be covered with a blanket of complete relaxation. Feel that relaxation as it reaches your forehead; feel the relaxation spreading to your cheeks, mouth, neck, and shoulders. Just feel those shoulders letting go and feeling so relaxed along with your arms, back, and abdomen down to your legs, feet, and even toes. You are now completely relaxed. You are feeling so comfortable now."

Dr. Kemper continued. "Raise your right index finger ever so slightly to show me you feel relaxed." Dr. Kemper smiled at Dorika's signs of total muscle relaxation that she could see in her face and on the GSR.

"Dorika, I want you to think of a happy place in your life. You mentioned being at the beach as being a relaxing place. This place should be where you feel warm and comfortable, without any fear. If it is at the beach, it is a lovely warm, sunny day with children playing and seagulls flying overhead. Nod your head slightly when you see your happy place," Dr. Kemper instructed.

Dorika nodded her head.

"Dorika, I'm going to show you a calendar. That calendar will go back in time to the day of the incident with Ambrus. Nod your head slightly if you see today's date, December 5, on the calendar."

Dorika nods her head.

"Now the calendar goes back in time slowly. It now reads November 30. It goes back slowly to November 26, when you came home from work. Remember, in hypnosis, you are always safe. If you start feeling any anxiety, you can stop being part of the scene and picture yourself as an observer of the scene below you. You can also go to your happy place for comfort if you have the need," reminded Dr. Kemper.

Dorika's breathing is still regular. The GSR indicates deep relaxation.

"Picture yourself coming home from work that day. Picture what happened at first. Tell me what happened." Dr. Kemper was taking notes.

"Went to nap," said Dorika.

"Then what happened?" asked Dr. Kemper.

"Ambrus home. He's mad. He pulls me out of bed onto the floor. Drags me up and throws me against the door frame."

Dr. Kemper notices an increase in Dorika's breathing rate and the lightening of her hypnosis state on the GSR. "Remember you are safe in hypnosis," says Dr. Kemper as Dorika's breathing accelerates. "Take some deep, relaxing breaths," Dr. Kemper requests. She asks Dorika to describe more of what happened when she is calmer.

"Ambrus throws me into the kitchen. I get up and grab the big knife," said Dorika.

"Take some deep relaxing breaths, become the observer when you need to," says Dr. Kemper.

"Ambrus looks afraid. He says he's going to take a shower. Talk later," Dorika says.

"Then what happens?" asks Dr. Kemper.

"I take the knife with me to the closet to get my backpack and sock with my money in it. I put the knife on the shelf so I can reach and take down my bag and money sock," Dorika says.

"You are doing great, Dorika. Deep breaths. Then what happens?" asks Dr. Kemper, encouraging her to continue.

"Ambrus comes up behind me. He's not in the shower. I have the bag and money sock. He grabs me and turns me toward him. Something stops him," says Dorika. "I don't know what happened, but I feel something wet. Ambrus lets go of me, and I run into the bathroom and lock the door. I put down my bag and money sock and put a chair under the doorknob."

"Okay, Dorika. You are safe. Deep breaths. How were you holding the bag and money sock?" Dr. Kemper asks.

"The bag was in my left hand, and the money sock in my right hand," says Dorika.

"What happens next?" asks Dr. Kemper.

"I yell out the window, 'Help, help, call the police.' Ambrus is banging on the door to the bathroom. Superintendent Randy is at the front door, yelling. I'm crouching on the floor," Dorika says, breathing more rapidly.

"You are doing great, Dorika. Take deep breaths. Know you are safe. What is happening now?"

"Ambrus is still banging on the bathroom door. Superintendent Randy says he's called the police. I hear sirens in the distance. I notice blood on my shirt," says Dorika.

"Deep breath. Feel that relaxation. What do you do now?" asks Dr. Kemper.

"There's no more knocking on the bathroom door. I check if I'm bleeding. Don't see any signs. I hear Superintendent Randy outside the bathroom, asking if I'm okay."

"That's great, Dorika. One more time about what happens next," says Dr. Kemper.

"I open the bathroom door. Superintendent Randy says Ambrus is gone from the apartment. I am safe," Dorika says.

"You did great, Dorika. We are going to bring you back to today's date on the calendar. See the calendar flipping slowly back to today, December 5. Get back that wonderful feeling of relaxation you felt at the beginning of this session. You can have that wonderful feeling any time when you put your index finger and thumb on your right hand together. When you come back fully, you will remember all that you said in this session. In a moment, I am going to count to five, and at number five, you will be relaxed and awake. One, starting to come back now; two, eyes starting to open; three, feeling good; four, almost fully alert; five, alert and relaxed."

Dorika opened her eyes like someone just waking from a deep sleep.

"How are you?" Dr. Kemper asked.

"Fine. I could not have stabbed Ambrus, right? I had my bag in one hand and my money sock in the other one," asked Dorika.

"That's what you saw, and that's what you said. I would suggest showing this video to your lawyer and getting him to interview Superintendent Randy. He can verify what you took into the bathroom with you. You did very well. Here's your copy of the video. I have an extra one here for anyone else who needs it or if they call me in to testify." Dr. Kemper handed Dorika the tape.

"Good luck, Dorika."

28

Dorika and Stan

Dorika left Dr. Kemper's office, smiling. Lynn was so pleased to see that.

"How did it go?" Lynn asked on the way down in the elevator to the car.

"I am so relieved," said Dorika. "I'll tell you in the car what happened. Maybe you can help me with what to do next."

In the car, Dorika detailed the hypnosis session and then the memory of the knife.

"I had put the knife down on the closet shelf when I went to get my bag and the money sock. I had my bag in my right hand and my money sock in my left hand when Ambrus grabbed me from behind and turned me around toward him. I couldn't have had the knife. He must have had it. I don't know exactly how Ambrus turning me around ended up with him stabbing himself in the stomach, but I didn't stab him," said Dorika, relieved.

"I am happy that you remembered what happened. Let's let the police figure out what happened based on the location and look of the wound. If I were you, I would call your lawyer and give him the tape. He'll work with the police," suggested Lynn.

"Yes, that's the right thing to do," said Dorika.

"I'm having dinner with Stan tonight. Is it okay with you if I tell him what you just told me?" asked Lynn.

"But of course. Stan has been so ready to help," said Dorika. "He seems like a nice person besides being a good policeman."

"That is true. Stan's a good guy," said Lynn.

Lynn met Stan at the *Island Café*. She decided not to have him pick her up at her brother's house. George was a wonderful brother, but the governor which monitored his actions, was not engaged when it came to her dates. *Dates,* she thought. *Am I having a real date with Stan?* Lynn grabbed a table by the window from which she could see Stan enter.

"You beat me here," said Stan. "I was hoping to be here first so you wouldn't be sitting alone," Stan said.

"One is never alone here. Plenty of seagulls and pelicans to keep one company. I just love watching them." Lynn thought how considerate Stan was. She enjoyed his company.

Stan appreciatively smiled at Lynn. He had always liked her caring, professional ways. Now he was seeing more of what she thought and felt about life in general.

"Have you ever been whale watching?" asked Stan.

"Just once a long time ago. I focused so much on school, work, and family in the last few years, a lot of the fun stuff got set aside," Lynn explained.

"Whale watching it is for a next adventure," said Stan. "Besides leaving Alan, you said you had other good news."

Lynn laughed. *Was Alan that bad and she hadn't seen it?*

"Dorika was hypnotized by Dr. Kemper yesterday. Thank you for that recommendation, by the way," Lynn shared.

"I hoped it turned out well for Dorika. She deserves some good news," Stan said.

"A strong yes. Dorika said it was okay for me to tell you what was on the tape. She thought it was the least she could do after you offered such valuable help."

"It was not a problem. It's what I do," said Stan.

"Dorika left the kitchen with the knife but put it down on the closet shelf when she went to take down her backpack and the sock with the money in it. She had something in each hand when Ambrus turned her toward him. Ambrus must have picked up the knife from the shelf. It must have plunged into his abdomen when he turned Dorika toward him," explained Lynn.

"Terrific. Where is that video of the session now?" asked Stan. "The sergeant in charge of her case could work that up. That's a great piece of info."

"Dorika was going to bring the video to her lawyer. She may have done it already. Dr. Kemper has a copy in case she needs to testify. She did suggest someone interview Superintendent Randy for his recollection of what Dorika was holding when she exited the bathroom," said Lynn.

"Great idea," said Stan.

"Dorika and I watched the tape at my brother's house. I noticed something on the tape. Dr. Kemper asked Dorika, 'How were you holding the bag and money sock?' She avoided saying, 'Was your bag in your right hand and your sock in your left hand' or something specific like that. She was meticulously careful not to imply certain information. I was impressed," said Lynn.

"Yep, that's what she does. She's exceptionally good at forensic hypnosis. So far, her part in all cases has been of assistance to defendants," Stan said.

The waiter was there to take their order.

"Wine or champagne?" asked Stan of Lynn.

"Usually I drink merlot. Champagne or prosecco would be great today," said Lynn.

"Bring us a bottle of your Moét & Chandon Impérial. We are celebrating," replied Stan.

Lynn smiled a little at Stan's choice of champagne. Alan would be shocked that a police detective would know about his favorite champagne.

"Shall we check out the menu? Have you had the she-crab soup here?" asked Stan.

When the waiter returned with their champagne, Lynn requested the she-crab soup and the broiled flounder with coleslaw and French fries on the side. She was starving. Stan also ordered the soup and the barbequed chicken with coleslaw and fries as well.

Stan held up his glass in a toast poise. "Here's to helping Dorika and to your new adventures."

"And here's to one terrific police detective and great friend," said Lynn.

"So, tell me about you," said Stan. We've worked together on several criminal issues, so I know you are smart. I remember you from when we lived in the same neighborhood. You were cute when you were small and gorgeous as you got older. By the way, where are you staying?"

"I'm currently staying with my brother and his family. George and his wife, Angie, have been terrific. As you know, George can be quite the character," said Lynn smiling.

"Oh, yes. George is a few years younger than me, but I remember some of his antics when we were in high school. Did you hear about the time he put a snake in a fellow's locker? George and this fellow liked the same girl. The snake was harmless but scared the pants off this other kid.

Maybe there was some weird note with the snake, something about this other boy being a snake in the grass. The teachers suspected George did it, but no one saw him or could prove it was him," Stan said.

"OMG," said Lynn. "I had heard about the snake in the locker story but never knew it was George that did it. I can't say I'm surprised," laughed Lynn.

"Are you doing okay with the split from Alan?" asked Stan.

"Oh, yes. Alan is not a bad guy. We are just incompatible. He's into the high-end lifestyle, which holds no appeal for me. My life is more focused on helping people who are ill or down and out, which has no appeal for Alan. Like I told him, there are plenty of women who would like the lifestyle he likes, and there's nothing wrong with wanting that. As far as I know, Alan is honest in his real estate dealings. We just disapproved of what each other wants."

Stan smiled. "Thank you for saying all that. I had been dating a little, and I met this genuinely nice woman. If she could come up with a socially acceptable way to ask, she would ask how much money I made and how much money I had in the bank. She also wanted to know if I would ever consider moving to a better part of town, maybe closer to the beach. My house is in Riverbanks, not exactly a shabby place," said Stan.

"Guess what? I'm buying a house in Dune Plantation. We will be in neighboring neighborhoods," said Lynn.

"More wonderful news," replied Stan. Both toasted their champagne glasses again.

29

Shandra

Shoreline Hospital System owns Deer Park Hospital and four other hospitals. Lynn had had a meeting with the other ED heads this morning at nine a.m. in Leland, North Carolina. She was heading back to Deer Park when she decided to stop at her favorite fast food place, McBurger's, for some chicken nuggets, french fries, and a diet Coke. She only treated herself to fast food when she did some traveling.

"What can I help you with this afternoon?" said a pleasant voice over the intercom. The voice sounded familiar.

"Six chicken nuggets, small fries, and a diet Coke," responded Lynn.

"That will be six nuggets, small fries, and I'm sorry, what to drink?" asked the voice.

"A diet Coke," said Lynn. *With all the innovations we have in this country, why can't they fix these intercoms so people can hear each other better?* Lynn thought.

"Thank you. That will be four seventy-five. Drive up to the first window, please."

Let's see what I have in my purse to pay with, thought Lynn. *Here's five dollars sitting next to twenty. I could give a tip to a fast-food employee who probably is lucky to make minimum wage.*

"That will be four seventy-five," said the woman at the window. Lynn guessed her to be in her middle to late thirties.

"Here you go. Here's a little something extra for the holidays," Lynn said. She handed the woman, whose name tag said Shandra, the five and the twenty-dollar bills. "Keep any change, too. "

"I don't understand," said Shandra. "You are giving me twenty dollars extra and want me to keep the change from the five? We don't do that here."

"I guess now you do, Shandra. Put the twenty dollars in your pocket, and if you would feel better, you can give me my twenty-five cents in change," suggested Lynn.

Shandra handed Lynn her receipt and a quarter. "I don't know what to say. Twenty dollars means a lot to me. My husband is out of work, and it has been tough. This job is the only income we have. I get eight dollars an hour, which doesn't go far, with two adults and two kids. This money may well be my only Christmas present. Thank you." Shandra's eyes were slightly wet as she talked.

"No, thank you for always being here at this window with a pleasant and a wonderful smile. It's not always easy to be friendly with cranky customers coming and going. I've been here before when you took my order and collected the money. You are always nice as pie. I'm also going to write to your company and suggest they encourage tipping. Restaurants do it. Why can't fast food places? You have a wonderful holiday."

"God bless and happy holidays to you, too," said Shandra.

Lynn drove to the next window and picked up her meal, which she always ate while returning to work.

SHANDRA PUT THE TWENTY DOLLARS IN HER POCKET. SHE had been working here at McBurger's for three years. No one had ever given her even twenty cents, never mind twenty dollars. *I can't cry now,* she thought. *Customers are waiting.*

"What can I help you with this afternoon?" Shandra said over the intercom. She tapped her pocket, checking if the twenty-dollar bill was still there.

Wow, thought Lynn. She had been handing out these twenties for the last few years. Shandra had touched Lynn at the core. *When I was in college,* she thought, *I did not have a lot of money. But I knew, someday, I would have a good job. What do people at McBurger's have to look forward to? Why don't we tip the fast-food staff? It wouldn't cost the management anything. That's how wait staff in restaurants make extra money on their low salaries.*

That evening at home, Lynn looked up tips for fast-food places. She could not find much written about tipping, but she did find how to contact the corporate office of McBurger's. She decided to write to them.

Dear Sir/Madam,

On a drive back to work, I stopped at a McBurger's for lunch. I gave the woman who took the order and processed my bill a twenty-dollar tip and wished her a happy holiday. At first, she was confused since no one tips at McBurger's. I insisted she take the twenty dollars. Then she touched my heart. She said her husband was out of work, and this twenty dollar bill would be her only Christmas present. It occurred to me that particularly during this holiday time, McBurger's could encourage customers to tip the staff. Eight dollars an hour does not go far, a pay increase would be terrific, but an extra dollar per customer could help a lot. Please consider it.

The next day Lynn received a response from McBurger's.

Hello Lynn,

Thank you for taking the time to contact McBurger's. We sincerely appreciate customer feedback and welcome the opportunity to share some information with you.

More than ninety percent of McBurger's U.S. restaurants are owned and operated by independent business people. As independent owners, McBurger's franchisees have the authority to make individual operating decisions as they relate to their McBurger's restaurant operations.

Again, thank you for contacting McBurger's. We hope to have the opportunity of serving you again soon.

Betsey

McBurger's Customer Contact Center

That's interesting, thought Lynn. *It's up to the customers to contact each local McBurger's owner. Maybe corporate needs another response.*

Dear Sir/Madam. This email is about Betsey's response to my suggestion during this holiday time that it would be good if McBurger's promoted tipping.

Betsey told me ninety percent of McBurger's restaurants are franchised, and the owners make their own decisions like tipping or not tipping. I am writing to say that it was good to know. However, I know your corporate office controls the type and quality of food served at the restaurants. Your corporate office still has some say. A note to all your franchise operations suggesting the owners consider allowing tipping might influence them to at least think about encouraging tipping during these times. Many of us would like to help others during the holidays. We are not millionaires able to donate large amounts of money, but we certainly could tip the workers at McBurger's.

Thanks for listening.

Lynn was disappointed when there was no answer to the second email. *Hopefully, someone took the message to heart,* she thought.

30

Theresa's Son David

Lynn was clearing her desk of a report she had just finished for the ED when she heard an ambulance arrive. The nurses were rushing to get a young boy into the trauma room. She listened to the pages for Dr. Denise Phillips, a neurosurgeon, and Dr. Peter Fry stat to the ED.

Oh, Oh, this is not a good sign, thought Lynn. She joined the rush of nurses to the trauma room. Peter was already there, checking the boy for injuries. Dr. Phillips was running down the hall. He joined the assessment team. It was then Lynn recognized Theresa standing just outside the door.

"Theresa, is this little boy David?" Lynn asked.

Tears were running down Theresa's face like a waterfall, which answered Lynn's question. She put her arms around Theresa's shoulder.

"Can you tell me what happened?" Lynn asked after a few minutes.

"David was riding his bike on the sidewalk in front of our house. He asked if he could ride it to the stop sign, which was about ten houses away. I said, yes. As he rode by one of the neighbor's houses, the man who lives there drove his car out of his garage and hit David with his car." Theresa took a few minutes to calm herself a little.

"I don't think the neighbor was going fast, but it happened so quickly, I'm not sure. David talked to us for a few minutes but then stopped. I'm so scared," said Theresa.

"Theresa, I know you are scared. Anyone would be. I can tell you the two doctors who are examining David are the best in their field. The nurses are super, too. Is your husband coming?" asked Lynn.

"He's on his way here from Charlotte. He was on a truck run there." Theresa sat, wiping the tears from her eyes, trying to stay in control of her fears.

"Let me go find out what is happening with David. I will be right back," Lynn said the last part very emphatically.

In the trauma room, Lynn could see the nurses had started intravenous fluids. David was hooked up to a cardiac monitor with a pulse oximeter on his finger to check his oxygen levels. He was breathing on his own, which Lynn took to be a good sign.

"How's he doing, Beatrice?" Lynn asked.

"He's still unconscious, but he's tried to open his eyes a few times. His vital signs are stable, and his oxygen level is good. We are thinking he's probably not bleeding, at least not profusely anywhere. We did a portable x-ray. It looks like he's got a fractured tibia. He's got bruises on his arm but no fractures. As soon as everyone is comfortable that he is stable, they will send him for a head scan. Dr. Phillips thinks he's had a concussion but wants to make sure there are no skull fractures or signs of bleeding in the brain." Beatrice was worried, Lynn could tell.

"Thanks. It seems hopeful David is going to be okay. Let me see if Dr. Fry will come and talk with his mother," Lynn said.

As if on cue, Peter came up to Lynn. "Hi," he says. "Do you know where the mother is?"

Lynn took Peter out to meet Theresa. They talked for a few minutes with Peter explaining what Beatrice had told Lynn.

"We are and will continue to take first-rate care of your son, Theresa. After he gets his head x-rayed, he will go to the pediatric ICU. That's just a precaution," Peter added quickly. "As soon as he's stable, we'll get a better x-ray of his leg to determine if I can just put a cast on or if he'll need surgery. From the portable x-ray, it looks like he might just need a cast, but I want to be sure. I'm a pretty picky surgeon," Peter added.

Theresa managed a small smile. "Thank you so much, both of you."

Peter pulled Lynn aside. "I think he's going to be fine, but I don't want to promise that until he's going out the door to his home."

"I understand. Thank you from me, too. Theresa is a good soul. She and her husband and son just moved here about a year ago."

"How do you know her?" Peter asked.

"She is one of my twenty-dollar recipients," Lynn explained.

"Well, then we need to have dinner so I can hear all about that. You free on Saturday?"

Lynn pretended to look through an invisible book. "Calendar says I'm cleaning the porch, so yes, I'm free," Lynn said, smiling.

"That's what I wanted to hear. Will you still be at George's house?"

"Good question. There's a possibility I might have moved into my new house. I'll text you with my whereabouts."

"You know I'll find you wherever you are," Peter said, grinning. "If we weren't in the middle of the ED, I'd give you a hug." Peter did manage to squeeze Lynn's hand.

"Looking forward to Saturday," Lynn said.

Lynn walked toward Theresa and the trauma room. *Hmm,* she thought. *Between Stan and Peter, my dance card is getting full. Having both of them as friends is fine. If things get serious, that might become a problem for all of us. Yikes.*

31

Moving and Alan

Lynn checked her messages when she got home. Angela had texted her about the closing on the house for Wednesday.

"Hi, Lynn. Glad you called," said Angela. We set the closing for nine a.m. on Wednesday. You do not need to come if you are working. I know your lawyer will be there."

"That sounds good. I'd like to go to work on Wednesday morning and then take the rest of the week off. The painters are coming on Wednesday afternoon and Thursday. I have tentatively scheduled my furniture delivery for Friday. I can take possession Wednesday afternoon, right?" asked Lynn.

"As soon as those papers are signed, the house is yours," replied Angela. "You can pick up the keys to the house at my office any time after the closing."

"Great. So far, this has been a smooth purchase. Do you see any black clouds on the horizon?" asked Lynn. She's learned no matter what one is involved in; there's usually something that holds up progress.

"We are still waiting on the inspection report. That should be in any time now. Sometimes, when people move out, and the house is empty, you can see problems that were covered up, intentionally or not, beforehand. On the inspection, I did have a client who found a number of the door frames had been damaged slightly by the owners' furniture movers. My client got an extra eight hundred dollars to fix those door frames."

"Okay, I'm convinced to make a move-out inspection. Can we do it at seven-thirty before the closing?" Lynn held her breath, waiting for Angela's reply at that early time.

"Sure, why not. I'll see you at the house at seven-thirty on Wednesday."

That's settled, thought Lynn. *I just need to call Alan to set a time for the movers to pick up the furniture on Friday.*

"Alan," Lynn said into his voicemail. "I'm just reconfirming I will be coming to the apartment to pick up my clothes and furniture on Friday. I'll be there at eight to get my clothes together and other stuff. The movers will be there at nine-thirty. I'll email you again the final list of pieces of furniture we agreed upon that I'd be taking with me. I hope you have a good day."

That should do it, thought Lynn. *I think I've covered everything on my to-do list!*

The phone rang. Lynn saw it was Alan calling her back. She hesitated for a minute, not wanting to talk with him but decided to answer.

"Hi, Alan," she said. "How's it going?"

"Can we meet? I just want to go over a few things with you," replied Alan.

I don't want to go over anything, Lynn thought.

"Can we do it over the phone?" asked Lynn.

"I'd like to see you. I'm cooking clams linguini. I know how much you like that dish. Come over for dinner," Alan suggested.

I might as well get it over with, thought Lynn. *I wish he could cook something besides clams linguini.*

"Okay, give me fifteen minutes," said Lynn, wondering what was on Alan's mind.

"See you then," said Alan.

Lynn tried to think about what Alan could want to talk over while driving to her old apartment. She tried to prepare for any type of argument. Lynn eliminated the furniture on her inventory as a potential dispute area. Despite Alan's bravado that he would buy new furniture for his new house, most of what she was removing was her furniture. The moving date should not be an issue. *So, what was so important, we had to meet?* she asked herself.

The door to the apartment was unlocked, so Lynn just walked in.

"I'm here," she said.

Alan looked good, Lynn thought. He was a handsome man—about six-one, medium brown hair, blue eyes. He had on a light blue shirt open at the neck, with a navy sweater vest. Alan hugged her.

"Thanks for coming over. Dinner is almost ready," said Alan. "What would you like to drink?"

"Just water is good for me, thanks." Lynn just had this uneasy feeling. It was the 'it's always something' feeling. She doubted it would be good news.

"I have some prosecco, which will be good with the dish," said Alan.

I'm not going to argue tonight. I just want to get this over with, thought Lynn.

"Sure, that sounds good," Lynn said.

Alan poured them both a glass. He raised both glasses, "Here's to new beginnings," he said.

"Dinner, as always, is delicious. So, what did you want to talk about, Alan?" asked Lynn.

"I was hoping you would reconsider moving out. I miss you. You are perfect for me."

Lynn sighed and gathered up some strength, from where she didn't know.

"Alan, we have been over this time and time again. I am not perfect for you. You try to remake me every opportunity you get. You want me to be perfect for you, but that's not reality," Lynn said with emphasis.

"I know I can be obnoxious at times. I have my ways, and you have yours. I don't want us to break up," Alan said, drinking down his second glass of wine.

Is it in the water this week? I didn't even change perfume. First, Peter, then Stan, and now Alan, thought Lynn.

"Alan, I can appreciate this split is not easy for you. It's not easy for me, either. But we are incompatible. It's just not working, and I do not want to keep trying to get it to work. I'm done. If you want to maintain a friendship, that's fine with me," said Lynn.

"Since we will still be friends, will you at least think about going with me to events?" asked Alan.

"What? You want me to be your plus one when you go out?" asked Lynn, appalled at the request.

So, this is it, thought Lynn. *It's not that he loves me or even likes me. I make a good impression at the real estate gatherings. Should have known.*

"Alan, I'm not available to be your plus one. That makes me look like I'm still your girlfriend. I'm starting a new life, and looking like your girlfriend won't help," replied Lynn, exasperated.

"So, you are seeing someone else already. Might have known you've been cheating on me." Alan sounded angry now. Lynn was a little worried.

Lynn got up from the table. She walked over to the closet to get her coat. Alan followed her and helped her on with her overcoat. As they faced each other, Alan bent down to kiss her.

"No, Alan. We are trying to be friends. It's not friends with benefits."

Lynn shut the door vigorously after she walked out of the apartment.

32
Work

THIS MORNING AT WORK, LYNN DID HER USUAL ROUNDS IN the ED. She could not believe being in the ED was less stressful than her personal life.

"Hi, John, how did it go last night?" she asked the night nurse, John Rubenstein.

"Pretty good, considering. There was a confrontation near the beach. One fellow got stabbed in the back. He got here quickly, and fortunately, the knife didn't hit any major blood vessels or nerves. The surgeons patched him right up.

"We still have one case of a twenty-four-year-old woman, Sylvia Vega, who Beatrice thinks might be a trafficked victim. Sylvia came in with an injured ankle, swollen and black and blue. The guy she came in with wanted to be with her all the time. He had all her ID info. We asked him to leave during her physical, but he gave us a hard time until the policeman stationed here walked by the room. She has multiple bruises, is exceptionally thin and quiet. The doctor ordered some blood work. We sent her down to x-ray and asked Mindy, the social worker who manages these cases, to see her there. They haven't come back yet. The guy she came in with was in the waiting area, but now he is gone."

"Keep me posted on that one," said Lynn. "I'm going to pediatrics to see David, the young boy who got hit by a car, but I'll be back soon."

The nurses had moved David out of the pediatric intensive care unit to the regular pediatric floor. Lynn was happy to learn about that. As she approached David's room, she heard voices. Dr. Pete was talking to David and his mother about a cast. Lynn decided to listen to their conversation before entering the room.

"Master David, we are ready to put your leg in a cast. What do you think about that?" asked Dr. Pete.

"Will it hurt?" asked David.

"I've never felt a thing when I put on a cast. Thanks for asking," replied Dr. Pete.

"Not you!" said David, laughing a little. "Will it hurt me?"

"So sorry, my mistake. I thought you were worried about me," said Dr. Pete smiling a little.

"No, you're a grownup. You can take care of yourself. I'm just a kid," replied David.

"I'm sure glad we got that straightened out," said Dr. Pete.

At this point, David, Theresa, and Dr. Pete were all laughing. Lynn was smiling, too, and admiring Peter's ability to make even the smallest patient feel relaxed.

"This cast won't hurt while being put on. The splint you have on your leg now has kept your leg straight. The cast is just stronger. We will make your cast to fit you. We make it out of fiberglass, the same stuff out of which boat builders make boats. Did you know that about boats?" asked Dr. Pete.

"Our neighbor has a boat. I'll ask him about that," replied David.

"Good idea. When you come to see me again, will you tell me what your neighbor says?"

"Sure," said David.

Lynn entered the room. "Good morning," she said.

Theresa hugged Lynn. "Thank you for everything. David is going to be okay. I'm so grateful for the excellent care from the doctors and nurses," said Theresa.

"We like Dr. Pete," piped up David.

Peter took a bow! "At your service, mate," he answered with a salute.

"I'm going to take this lovely nurse out to speak with her for a moment. I'll be back later," said Dr. Pete.

"Hi, Lynn," said Peter. "Good to see you. We were able to line up the fractured tibia with the splints. He'll have a cast for three to four weeks, and then he'll be good as new. Kids are great healers."

"You were so amazing with David, a superstar when it comes to working with kids," said Lynn.

Well, thank you. David is incredibly charming. We still on for Saturday? Do you know where you are going to be?" asked Peter.

"Definitely yes for Saturday. If everything goes well, I'll be in my new house. Might be a lot of boxes around, though," said Lynn.

"Boxes! Yay, I love boxes. I cut them up with my saw, only after emptied, of course. I can help if you need help," Peter volunteered.

"Thank you—kind of you to offer. I'll text you my new address and let you know if I'm going to be there. Dinner will be a wonderful break to look forward to," said Lynn.

"I'm counting the days until dinner." Peter squeezed Lynn's elbow.

Lynn spent a few minutes more talking with Theresa and David. Since they were in good hands, she went back to the ED. She found Beatrice Tucker.

"Beatrice, how are we doing with Sylvia Vega?"

"Mindy did get a chance to talk with her. One of the Romeo pimps seduced her from Miami. He used the usual flowers, presents, and 'you are beautiful' routine. He drove her up here under the guise of meeting his family. Instead, she became part of the sex trade that's online. Romeo turned her over to one of the Gorilla pimps who beats her if she doesn't do what he wants her to do. It's so horrifying," says Beatrice.

"That was a good pickup on your part, Beatrice. Was Sylvia okay with notifying the police?"

"Yes, for sure, and with contacting A Safe Place. Mindy says she's traumatized but has the strength to get away. Thank goodness North Carolina doesn't charge these victims with prostitution. The police are out looking for her handler. He left the bottle of water I gave him. I gave that to the police, too," said Beatrice.

"Smart move on your part. Fingerprints will help a lot. You do good work, Beatrice," said Lynn. She made a mental note to add all this to Beatrice's performance review.

"We all are getting better at identifying these trafficked victims and getting evidence for the police. The courses you made available to take, plus the numerous unfortunate experiences with these cases, help us better at finding cases. Although we still want to beat up the pimps, given how evil they are," replied Beatrice. "Soapsuds enemas for all of them."

"Thank you for such a good job and letting the police handle the traffickers. They can be dangerous." Lynn said. She understood how hard it was to see the physical and emotional damage done to these victims.

"Sylvia now has a better life because of you," Lynn said, touching Beatrice's arm.

33

Moving and Shandra

LYNN STOOD IN THE MIDDLE OF THE EMPTY LIVING ROOM OF her new house. The living room, breakfast nook, and kitchen were one big, open room. The sun shown through just enough to bring in a warm glow. She loved it already. Satisfied, she left quickly to meet the movers at her old apartment.

"Hi," said Alan. "This is a sad day for me."

It was always about Alan. You'll get over it, thought Lynn. "I'll have you over for dinner after I unpack everything. Remember, we agreed to remain friends."

"Sounds good. I'm happy to bring food, too. Your cooking is not the best," said Alan.

Thank goodness, I'm leaving, thought Lynn. *No more putdowns.*

"That will be fine," Lynn replied.

The movers arrived.

"Shandra, is that you?" Lynn said, recognizing that the woman with the moving crew was the one from the McBurger window.

"Hi! Aren't you the woman who gave me the twenty dollars?" replied Shandra.

"That would be me. I'm Lynn."

Shandra gave Lynn a big hug. "This is my husband, Booker." Booker was tall, maybe six-two, and muscular. He towered over Shandra, who was five-four at most.

"So, you two are in the moving business, now?" asked Lynn.

"It's us three. Let me introduce you to Billy, our friend. He got us this job. And you helped, too."

"Really? How was that?" asked Lynn.

"You probably don't remember I mentioned my husband was out of work when you gave me the twenty dollars. Billy called and said there was this job opening with this moving company. Booker had to get a bunch of papers together and overnight them to the company in Charlotte."

Lynn was beginning to understand.

"When I came home from McBurger's the day I met you, Booker told me all this. He had called around. To copy all the papers and overnight them was going to cost about eighteen dollars. 'Eighteen dollars that we do not have,' he said."

Lynn nodded. "Go on."

"I reached into my pocket and handed him the twenty dollars. 'Merry Christmas,' I said. He's a big guy, as you can see, but just between you and me, he cried."

"Glad I could help," said Lynn. It was sad for her, though, to know eighteen dollars stood between applying for a job or not. "Are you still at McBurger's?"

"Oh, yes. I do this part-time. Here, I do the math part, labeling and counting the boxes and furniture, billing, and light lifting, too, as needed," explained Shandra. "By the way, my boss at McBurger's has placed a tipping jar on the counter and a sign on the window stations saying tipping is allowed."

"That's great news, Shandra. Thanks for telling me that," said Lynn.

"Yeah, he said corporate sent a memo to all McBurgers suggesting they allow tips during the holidays especially," Shandra elaborated.

"We better get the moving going," said Booker. "Mr. Alan is starting to look agitated."

"Alan," Lynn called out to him. "I'm going to show them what they will be moving. I have everything labeled, but I want to show them."

"Come here, you two," said Lynn. She brought Shandra and Booker into the bedroom.

"Alan is a real estate agent. I think if you showed him how careful you are and agree with everything he says, you might get some referrals from his clients," Lynn said in a low voice.

"Gotcha, Ms. Lynn," said Shandra. "I'm good with customers."

"Yes, you are, Shandra. Yes, you are." Lynn agreed.

"You know we will be extra careful with all your belongings, too," said Booker.

"Thank you," said Lynn.

Shandra left the room. "Mr. Alan," she said. "Here's the list Ms. Lynn gave me. Here is how we are going to proceed, so you know. We do everything to protect the furnishings we are moving, those that are staying, and of course, the walls of the apartment. Let us know if you have any concerns. We pride ourselves at always leaving satisfied customers."

Way to go, Shandra, thought Lynn. She also appreciated the irony of the situation where Alan could also help one of her twenty-dollar recipients.

The move out of the apartment and into Lynn's new home went off without a dent, scratch, or crack.

George stopped in to see Lynn's new house on his way home. The movers had left with the furniture set up and in place. The guest room had no furniture, so it held all the boxes except for the kitchen supplies. There was only a stuffed chair in the living room, but the kitchen table and chairs were near the window overlooking the flowers in the front of the house.

"Would you like some tea or coffee?" Lynn asked George.

"I was hoping for something stronger," laughed George.

Lynn poured him a glass of Glenlivet Scotch over ice.

"There is a reason you are my favorite sister," said George.

"I'm your only sister," replied Lynn.

"Well, if I had others, you would still be my favorite," answered George. "I've got Mom on speed dial in case you poke me again."

"So, what do you think of the place?" asked Lynn.

"It's you! The big thing is Alan isn't here. Hurray! But seriously, I like it." George looked around, admiring the rooms.

Lynn filled George in on the movers and the possibility Alan could end up recommending one of her twenty-dollar recipients to his clients.

"That's the story that made my day today. There's one more thing," said George.

"Yes, and what would that be?" asked Lynn.

"Angie and I would like to buy you a couch as a housewarming gift if that's okay with you."

"That's too much," said Lynn. "A potted plant would be good. I understand snake plants don't need much care and help clean the air."

"Now listen to me, your big brother. You know we can well afford to buy you a couch. Plus, that way, I can feel comfortable coming over and sitting on it when I need to. We'll throw in the snake plant. Snake plant? Does it crawl around?" asked George.

"You do know you have one in your living room, silly," said Lynn.

"That thing is a snake plant? Wow. Angie snuck that one in on me. Okay, then a couch and a snake plant. Do we have a deal?" asked George

"Sounds good. Thank you, and you can come and occupy the couch whenever you want. Love you, bro."

34

Stan and Dorothy

AFTER GEORGE LEFT, LYNN RAN TO THE GROCERY STORE. There was a Harris Teeter about two miles away in one direction and a Whole Foods in the opposite direction, the same distance. *All these new experiences*, thought Lynn. She headed for Harris Teeter as her first run.

As she headed down to the vegetable and fruit section, she heard a familiar voice, "Hi, there," said Stan. "Nice to see you, neighbor, in our neighborhood grocery store."

"This is like being on Mr. Roger's show," said Lynn. *If I'm going to be bumping into people I know here, I better dress better,* thought Lynn. *What are the odds of me being here at the same time as Stan, although it is the end of most people's workday?*

"Yes, it is a beautiful day in the neighborhood to bump into you. How's moving going?" asked Stan.

"It went very well. The movers delivered all my stuff today. I'm just unpacking and getting food. It will take a while to get settled in, but so far, I love the house and the area," said Lynn.

"And the neighbor?" asked Stan.

"But of course. It's comforting to have a police detective friend so close. It makes me feel secure."

"I am at your service at any time. Do you need help unpacking?" asked Stan. "How about I cook you dinner?"

"Dinner would be lovely, but maybe in a few more days. I want to get the house in shape before I go back to work on Monday. It's going to be old jeans and sweatshirts for the next two days."

"How about next Tuesday? I'll text you my address. Around seven?" asked Stan.

"That would be great. Thanks. Good to see you, neighbor," said Lynn.

After Lynn unpacked her groceries, she texted Peter, saying she would be in her new house from now on. She sent the address and told him she was looking forward to dinner.

He sent a text back with a large picture of a flower bouquet.

Then Lynn called her mom.

"Hi, Mom," Lynn said.

"How are you, sweetheart?" asked Dorothy.

"I'm doing fine and getting settled into my new house. The move went well. I have to tell you about the third person to whom I gave a twenty-dollar bill," said Lynn. She told her mother about giving Shandra the twenty dollars while she was working the window at McBurgers.

"She and her husband and another fellow were my movers. I didn't tell them I had seen Shandra's picture on the ad for the moving business for which she and her husband worked. I acted surprised to see them. Shandra told me they used the twenty dollars to overnight a job application for her husband. Things were tough for them," Lynn said.

"What a great story! Thank you so much for continuing the twenty-dollar tradition. It's the best holiday gift of all for me," said Dorothy, a little nostalgic about not being able to hand out the twenty-dollar bills herself.

"I haven't told you the best part yet," said Lynn.

"I pulled Shandra and her husband, Booker, aside and told them about Alan being a real estate agent. I suggested if they talked with him about what a super, conscientious job they do and agree with everything he says, they might get some referrals. Shandra picked up on that immediately and had a splendid conversation with Alan."

"You know I have always held your brother responsible for the trouble and fights that happened. Now I'm seeing more of the devil in you," said Dorothy.

"Mom, you need to see how delicious that was. Alan always complained about you and me giving out these twenty-dollar bills during the holiday. 'They should be getting better jobs,'" Lynn said, mimicking Alan.

Dorothy laughed. "I can hear him now."

"I'm just agreeing with Alan and letting him arrange work for one of the twenty-dollar recipients. I know they do good work. This is a win-win for everyone," said Lynn. Alan looks in the know to his customers, Shandra and Booker get more jobs, and I have the joy of knowing Alan is involved in our plot to make lives better for others." Lynn's voice had an edge of joy and innocence to it.

"That devil in you is more at play than I thought; however, I agree everyone wins. Okay, mischief-maker and goody two shoes at the same time, good going. You are even better at this twenty-dollar handout than I was," said Dorothy. "Speaking of which, any further news about Dorika?" asked Dorothy.

"That seems to be clearing up nicely. Dorika's lawyer brought the hypnosis tape to the DA. She decided between the abuse and Ambrus not taking proper care of his cut that Dorika won't be charged with anything. Everything needs to go through probate, but she can just take anything in the apartment they shared right away, including the fifty thousand dollars."

"What about the rest of the money? Wasn't there about four hundred and fifty thousand in the bank?" asked Dorothy.

"That's still unresolved. The police and the DA are mulling that over, according to the lawyer. If Ambrus got that money illegally, the police might confiscate it. Because he's dead, they can't prosecute him, so they have to decide if it's worth their time and resources to find out where Ambrus got the money," Lynn explained.

"I'm happy she isn't abused anymore and has some money to help her start over. She's so sweet," said Dorothy.

"Speaking of sweet. I think Randy, the superintendent, has feelings for Dorika. He seems like a nice guy. He's taking good care of her, too. To be continued," said Lynn.

"I will sleep well tonight with all this good news. Goodnight, sweetheart. Love you," said Dorothy.

"Goodnight, Mom. Love you, too."

35

Lynn Meets Lucas

LYNN WAS UP EARLY THE NEXT DAY, READY TO FACE EMPTYING the boxes.

First coffee and some toast, she thought. *No, I couldn't have forgotten to get butter. It's always something.*

Lynn ran into the Harris Teeter, straight to the refrigeration section where the store kept the butter.

She debated between waiting at the self-check area, which was full, or going to the full-service line, which had no one behind the fellow checking out. She chose the full-service line. Lynn soon realized why that line was so short. The man now in front of her was putting food back, apparently short of enough cash to buy everything he picked up.

The man looked to be in his thirties. His overall appearance was of someone down and out. He had on a frayed shirt, jeans that fit loosely, and a face full of worry. He was buying baby formula, diapers, and adult food, like milk, eggs, bread, ground beef, chicken, and fruit.

How am I going to handle giving this man twenty dollars to help pay for his groceries? Lynn thought. From her experience handing out twenty-dollar bills, men were less inclined to take money from her. She had an idea, but she needed the cashier's help. She caught the cashier's eye and winked at her. The cashier gave her a slight nod.

Okay, she's in on it, thought Lynn.

Lynn took a twenty-dollar bill out of her pocket and bent down to the floor. When she got up, she tapped the man in front of her on the shoulder.

"Sir, did you drop this?" Lynn asked, holding the twenty-dollar bill.

"I don't think so. Maybe it's yours," the man answered back.

"No, I know it's not mine. All my cash is in my wallet," Lynn said. She turned to the cashier. "Do you have a lost-and-found section here? I'm new to this store."

"We do, but money, honestly, rarely gets returned. People can't prove the money was theirs like they can with things. I'd suggest one of you keep it," said the cashier. Lynn's love of the neighborhood just grew some more.

Lynn turned to the man. "I know this twenty-dollar bill is not mine. I'm also in a hurry. If you take it, we can both get out of the store quicker. What about it?" Lynn asked.

The man looked at Lynn and then the cashier. He smiled. "Works for me," he said. He gave the cashier the twenty dollars. She quickly finished ringing up and packing the man's groceries, sending him on his way.

"Thank you for doing that," said the cashier, whose name tag read Sandra.

"Thank you for helping, Sandra."

"I know this man. He's a good guy. His name is Lucas Hungler. His wife just had a baby, but something went wrong. Something went into her blood—it wasn't a clot but something else," said Sandra.

"An amniotic fluid embolism?" asked Lynn.

"That sounds right. The wife, Sydney, is still in the hospital, barely alive. The doctors are not sure she's going to make it. It's such a sad situation," Sandra said.

"That is tragic," said Lynn. "So, he's taking care of the baby?"

"He and his mother, who helps out. "She's not well, either. He had to take time off from work to be with the baby. I don't know if he's getting paid or not—it seems like money is tight," said Sandra, sharing her observation.

"Sounds like you know them pretty well," commented Lynn.

"They come into the store a lot, and I went to high school with Sydney. It's a small world around here. My friends and I try to help out, but Lucas is a proud guy," said Sandra.

"I see. I know from other experiences, cashiers are discouraged from giving money to customers who can't pay for the groceries. Is that the same here?" asked Lynn.

"Yes, it's the same here but flexible, especially during the holidays. Thank you again," Sandra said. She bagged Lynn's butter and focused her attention on the next customer standing in line.

Lynn headed back home. Her thoughts were still with Lucas Hungler and his baby and his wife. It is hard when something beautiful is supposed to happen, but it turns out to be a tragedy. On the drive home, she thought about boxes that needed emptying and dinner tonight with Peter. She realized how lucky she was.

36

Lucas

As Lucas entered his apartment, he could hear Lucy crying. Much to her apparent dismay, having her diaper changed by her grandmother lacked comfort and appeal. Lucas put the groceries down in the kitchen.

"How's everything going?" he asked his mother.

"She's the wiggliest baby I've ever known. Just when I think I've got this diaper on, she wiggles around. There! Now it is on. Wow!"

Lucas held Lucy while his mother, Elizabeth, disposed of the diaper. Lucas could never have imagined feeling the love he had for this baby. He held her on his shoulder, where he could feel her nuzzling against his neck. Lucas knew that was a sign she was looking for breast milk. He went to the kitchen to heat the formula for her.

"Lucas, do you want me to put away the groceries? I can stay a while longer," asked Elizabeth.

"If you would just put the eggs, milk, and chicken in the fridge, that would be helpful. I can do the rest after I feed Lucy. Thank you for all your help, Mom."

"It's my pleasure. I wish I could do more. Are you going to the hospital later on?" asked Elizabeth.

"The doc's going to call me this afternoon. I'm going to see what he says about Sydney's condition," Lucas replied.

Elizabeth put on her coat and came over to hug Lucas. "Love you, son."

"Right back to you, Mom," said Lucas.

Lucas sat in the rocking chair his mother had given him and fed Lucy her bottle. His thoughts wandered from money issues, taking care of Lucy, his job, and his dying wife. Tears filled his eyes. He had never felt so desperate.

"Crying isn't going to help," Lucas said to himself. "Think, man, how are you going to handle all that's on your plate."

He put Lucy on his shoulder to burp her. For such a little creature, she sure had a loud burp. She looked up to him with big dark eyes. The nurses said it would take several months before he'll know Lucy's permanent eye color. He hoped they would be the exquisite blue color like Sydney's. Tears filled his eyes again.

"Man, stop this. Start working on figuring out what to do," he said out loud. Lucy had fallen asleep in his arms, so he put her in her crib. She looked so content and restful without any worries. He hoped he could keep her life that way.

"Get ready for the doctor's call," he said to himself. He looked over the sheet of information about Sydney the nurses gave him.

Oxygen level was eighty-eight—low, they warned. That was with the ET tube they said was in her trachea attached to a ventilator. The chest x-ray showed fluid in her lungs, the docs referred to as pulmonary edema. Her heart function, so far, was doing okay, except for a fast heart rate. She was also unconscious.

The doctor had said most women do not survive an amniotic fluid embolism. If they do, they are in the hospital and rehab for months and have neurological problems.

The only good news, the doc said, was they treated Sydney early and were able to maintain her blood pressure and reduce any bleeding.

The phone rang.

"Hello," said Lucas.

"Lucas, this is Dr. Henry. How are you doing?"

"As well as could be expected, I guess," said Lucas.

"I have a little bit of good news. Your wife's oxygen level has moved up to ninety-two percent. The number, while important, is not as significant as the direction of the oxygen level. We see progress instead of decline," said Dr. Henry.

"Do you think she might make it, Doc?" asked Lucas.

"It's too early to tell. I do have a suggestion, though. We encourage all family and close friends and our staff to talk to patients when they are unconscious. We know from research; many unconscious patients can hear but not respond. Hearing the voices of loved ones is therapeutic besides being comforting," Dr. Henry said.

"I'm going to feel funny talking to Sydney as if she was awake," Lucas replied.

"Think about it. We don't want to overwhelm Sydney with visitors, but family and friends are welcome. In your wife's case, talking about the baby would be particularly beneficial. I've had family members record their baby's sounds."

"I don't have a good recorder," said Lucas. "Never got an upgraded cell phone that did that well."

"As I said, think about doing that. Do you have any questions, Lucas?"

"Is there anything else I can do to help my wife get better?"

"Right now, even being there with her, maybe holding her hand will be helpful. As we move through her recovery, we'll add more to your list."

"Thanks, Doc," said Lucas.

"Don't hesitate to ask the nursing staff or me any questions. Take care of yourself, too," said Dr. Henry, signing off.

Lucas sat down with a cup of coffee and a bagel. He was thankful for the woman who found the twenty dollars in the grocery store. He would have had to put back these bagels if she hadn't been there. Now he had to work on his finances. He was on leave from his job as a groundskeeper for a local landscaper. They had sick pay for their employees, but no paid sick leave if someone in the family was ill.

At least he still had health insurance for the next two weeks while not working, that covered him, Sydney, and now Lucy. But there was no money coming in. He needed to go back to work. But who would take care of Lucy then? His mother had irregular heartbeats, which caused her to be dizzy and unsteady at times, and had terrible arthritis. Who could he get to take care of his precious baby?

37

Dinner with Peter

Lynn quickly put away the groceries and started emptying boxes. She was beginning to remember how much work was involved in moving. This time felt different to her. She was happy with the house and her life in general. She understood better what she wanted and didn't like, especially in her relationships with men.

While happy with that part of her life, she was fighting the need to call her midwife friend, Wanda Houston, to find out about Lucas's wife.

"No one asked you to get involved," she said to herself out loud. To stop thinking about Lucas and his wife and baby, she put off checking on Sydney until Monday. She needed the weekend for herself. This weekend she was Lynn Price, homeowner, daughter, sister, and friend; her ED director self was on vacation.

Lynn had emptied the kitchen and dining room boxes. Now she was on to the bedroom. Besides unpacking, she needed to decide what to wear to dinner with Peter.

Is the red dress too much? she asked herself. *They were going to a nice restaurant. What message did she want to send to Peter? A better question, how did she feel about Peter? Did she want to be more than a friend?*

Five outfits later, she had decided on a dressy red sweater with a black leather skirt and boots. *Fashionable and a little sexy but not over the top*, she thought.

By seven-fifteen, Lynn had the kitchen, dining room, living room, and bedroom unpacked and liveable. Her office had her desk and computer set up, but her boxes were still unpacked. The spare room was full of boxes. She was dressed and had fifteen minutes before Peter arrived to give herself a once over. She was both nervous and happy about this real date.

The doorbell rang. *Calm down*, Lynn said to herself, as her heart beat faster. *It's just Peter.*

She opened the door and immediately thought Peter looked great.

"Hi. These are for you," Peter said, handing Lynn a mixed bouquet.

"They are lovely. Thank you," said Lynn. "Come on in and check out my new home."

"I just need to know if you saved me some boxes," laughed Peter.

"You need to use your imagination and visualize this couch next to that chair." Lynn handed Peter the picture of the couch she, George, and Angela had picked out.

"Exquisite," said Peter. "Considering you just moved in, the place looks great. Are you happy here?"

"I love this house. The house and I are going to live happily ever after," said Lynn.

"Hmm. I like the happily ever after part," said Peter. "You look lovely, by the way. I'm a lucky man to be taking you to dinner."

"How brave are you feeling tonight?" asked Peter walking from the parking lot to the restaurant.

"Brave? Oh, oh. Is this a dangerous place to eat?" asked Lynn.

"Here's the deal. There is indoor seating with a peek-a-boo view of the ocean. There is also porch seating with enclosed transparent curtains and heaters with outstanding views of the water. It might be a little chillier on the porch, though." Peter was hoping for the view since it was more romantic.

"So, I'm choosing between warmth or a fabulous view. Correct?" asked Lynn.

"Pretty much," said Peter.

"I'm good with the view if that works for you, too," responded Lynn.

For Lynn, saying this was a fabulous view was an understatement. The porch hung out from the main seating area closer to the ocean cove. There was a lighthouse on the left at the end of the jetty. The beams from the tower lit up the ocean waves as they crashed against the shore. On the right side, where the boats were docked, a lonely pelican sat motionless on a wooden piling.

"What would you like to drink, Lynn?" asked Peter.

"The prosecco we had before was delicious."

"Prosecco, it is." Peter gave the order to the waiter. "Should we look over the menu, so then we can talk," suggested Peter.

After a quick look over, Lynn decided on the clam chowder and the crab cakes with asparagus. She put the menu down the same time Peter did. They both laughed.

"Lynn, I need to tell you how great it is to see you almost every day at the hospital. First of all, you are gorgeous, but I also love how you manage the ED. The nurses and other staff are happy there. It's like a family that likes each other and works in harmony. That's you! That's how you are," said Peter.

"Well, thank you. That's nice of you to say. I can't take all the credit, though. There's this orthopedic doc who brings me coffee a lot," said Lynn. "He gets me through the day."

"When I come to the ED, I relax. Can you imagine? It's more relaxing to be in the ED, where people are banged up and bleeding than it is to be on the general surgical floors," said Peter.

"I'm getting embarrassed," said Lynn. "Next time I get into trouble with someone, I'm sending them to talk with you." Lynn smiled at Peter.

"No embarrassment. You need to be proud of the work you do," insisted Peter.

"It's a team effort. You are part of that team, too. Look at the fantastic way you talked to David. I loved watching you," said Lynn.

The waiter came with the prosecco and took their orders. Peter poured them each a glass of wine.

"Here's to both of us!" he said. "You know, seeing you and chatting, even if it's just a few minutes in the morning, makes me happy, happier than I've been in a long time."

"Glad to oblige. You always leave me smiling, too, when you visit," replied Lynn.

"Tell me more about you. What else, besides work and me, are important to you?" asked Peter.

38

Lucas

Lynn spent most of Sunday emptying boxes and organizing her new house. She also spent a lot of time thinking about Peter. She went over much of their conversation, mostly what had made them laugh. They had always worked well together, with an intuitive understanding of each other. Last night was different. She was with Peter, the person, not the doctor, and maybe the suitor. He had kissed her gently and warmly good night. He joked it was going to be hard for him to keep from kissing her at the hospital.

Monday morning had come quickly. Today was the day she would check on Lucas Hungler's wife, and after work, she was going to have dinner with her mother.

"Good Monday morning to you all," Lynn said. It was their monthly Monday morning staff meeting.

"Here's my list of items for today. Does anyone have something else to add?" No one added to the plan.

"Number one on my list is the addition of two new nurses to our staff. They will be starting next Monday in orientation. Bill has agreed to precept David Coswell when he's off the human resources orientation. I still need a preceptor for Carol Patterson. Anyone interested can see me after the meeting. I have passed out the list of new equipment coming in this week. All our equipment wishes went through as requested." There was clapping from the staff.

"Santa came early to the Deer Park ED," commented Lynn. "Who wants to go next?"

The staff brought up issues they were facing in their roles. The most significant cases concerned patients who had overdosed. There was an increase in patients who had overdosed because of suicide attempts, but the incidence of overdoses from street drugs had gone down. The staff nurses asked for reports on the actual number of suicide overdoses and the best practice treatments for those patients.

"I'll put that on my to-do list," said Lynn. "Great pickup, by the way."

Back in her office, Lynn called her friend, Wanda, the clinical nurse specialist in the hospital's maternity section.

"Hi, Lynn. How's it going?" asked Wanda.

"Good," said Lynn. "Busy as ever. But I'm calling for a favor."

"Shoot," Wanda said. "I'm sure I owe you at least five of them. My staff is now calling your ED the new admission center for maternity. Why do they wait so long to come in when they are in labor? What can I do for you?"

"I made the acquaintance of Lucas Hungler the other day. I heard his wife is in the hospital with an amniotic fluid embolism. Do you have time to have a chat with me about her?"

"Sure. I know Sydney. Come on up. I'm in my office," said Wanda.

"I'll be right there," replied Lynn. She told Beatrice, who was in charge today, where she would be.

"You want some coffee?" asked Wanda when Lynn arrived.

"That would be terrific. So how is Sydney Hungler doing, if I can ask?" said Lynn.

"Sure, if you keep it to yourself. Sydney came in through the ED, so she's one of your patients, too. All I can say anyway is she's still with us but on a vent. She's not getting worse, and maybe her oxygen level is up a little. I know the docs are trying a new combination of drugs today that have only been used a few times. They got the okay from the pharmacy and therapeutics committee to use the drugs. What's your concern?" asked Wanda.

"I think the husband is struggling not only with his wife so sick, but also financially. He had to take a leave from his job to take care of the baby. He's mucho stressed," said Lynn.

"You think a social worker could help?" asked Wanda.

"It's worth a shot. Lucas is a local guy who went to high school here. Some of those classmates might be willing to help out, from what I've heard," said Lynn.

"That's good to know. I'll send a referral to Rosa Morales, and she's a whiz at getting help for spouses with baby care and financial issues. We have some clunkers in this hospital, but the good ones are super-stars. Don't you think, Lynn?" asked Wanda.

"For sure. The clunkers should be assigned just limited space within which to roam. Thank you, my friend," said Lynn

"Any time. Let's do lunch soon, even if it's in the cafeteria."

"It's a date," said Lynn.

"Wait a minute. Speaking of dates, what's this I hear about you and Dr. Pete?"

"What? The hospital grapevine puts Google to shame. What have you heard?" asked Lynn.

"I heard you and Alan split and that you and Dr. Pete are dating," replied Wanda.

"I didn't think my personal life was important enough to make the grapevine circuit. For the moment, Peter and I are good friends, is all I'm saying for the rumor mill," said Lynn. "I can fill *you* in at lunch."

"Looking forward to that lunch," replied Wanda. "What's excellent in this hospital is the informal network like our chat. I know if I need a lab result in a hurry, I can promise Dave in the lab some cookies, and those results are on my computer in a flash! The administration thinks they run the place, but it's us worker bees that get the job done with our informal network."

"So, what kind of cookies does Dave like?" asked Lynn laughing.

39
Mom

LYNN LEFT WORK HAPPY. IT WAS A FULFILLING DAY BETWEEN the staff meeting and the conversation with Wanda. IT was going to keep track of the overdoses in the ED and send her weekly reports. She contacted the online nursing CE provider with whom the hospital has a contract. The provider is willing to develop a course on best practices for the care of a patient with an overdose from a suicide attempt. Wando sent her an email saying Rosa Morales has already spoken to Lucas with an emoji indicating everything was AOK.

Her mother had the table set for their dinner. "What's on the menu for tonight?" asked Lynn.

"We are having barbequed chicken with sweet potato fries and snap peas with a piece of cheesecake for dessert," said Dorothy.

"Are we celebrating something?" asked Lynn.

"Yes, we are. We are celebrating your new life with your new house. I'm immensely proud of you! Plus, I want to hear all about your date with Dr. Pete and the latest twenty-dollar recipients. We have a lot of ground to cover," said Dorothy.

Lynn laughed. "Do you have a preferred order for this discussion?"

"Let me think. Let's do your house first," requested Dorothy.

"I brought my computer so you can see it. I'm still organizing the inside, but that's working out well. George and Angie are getting me a couch and a plant. George wouldn't take no for an answer." Lynn opened her computer to her pictures.

"Good that George and Angie did that. You two kids have turned out very well," said Dorothy proudly. "Your house looks lovely. It seems like it would suit you. The apartment with Alan seemed way too formal. This is a home instead of a castle. While we are eating, tell me about your date with Dr. Pete," said Dorothy.

"It was great. We have had lunch and dinner together before but usually under the guise of work. What we had was a real date. Peter is such a great guy. He brought me flowers, and we had reservations at the *Harborview*. We talked and laughed a lot. I do like him, but we are just getting to know each other outside of work. Being with him left me with a warm feeling," said Lynn.

"I am delighted. George has such great things to say about him. I remember him from when he and George were in high school together. I'm sure he's matured into a fine man," said Dorothy.

"That he has. I have other news, too, but you cannot say anything to George. Promise?" asked Lynn.

"But of course."

"I am having dinner with Stan tomorrow night. He lives in the next neighborhood. We even bumped into each other at the grocery store," said Lynn.

Dorothy looked seriously at Lynn, then started to laugh. "My daughter, the popular, beautiful, young woman. Good for you. Stan is a wonderful guy, too. Wow."

"Right now, I'm not taking anything too seriously. We will see how it all plays out," said Lynn.

"I do have some news and some questions about the twenty-dollar recipients. "Do you remember Theresa, the woman who couldn't afford the toy for her son that I met in the toy store?"

"Oh, yes, that was such a great story. Wasn't Theresa's husband a hero because of his actions during a truck and car accident?" asked Dorothy.

"Yes, that's the one. Their son, David, got hit by a car and came into the ED. He's doing fine. Peter was the one who put a cast on his leg. I stood outside the door, watching Peter establish a relationship with David. Peter was funny, caring, and just amazing with him," said Lynn.

Dorothy looked at her daughter light up as she talked about Peter. She so hoped Lynn would find a first-rate partner.

"The second person I gave the twenty-dollar bill to, Dorika, seems to be doing fine now. As you know, the ADA cleared her of knifing Ambrus, and won't be pressing charges or taking her to court. They are not even going to investigate the money Ambrus had obtained. It all went to Dorika."

"Dorika stops in now and then and updates me. She's so happy now. Did you know she and Superintendent Randy are dating?" asked Dorothy.

"No way! Stan thought he liked her, but I didn't know about the dating. Life takes happy turns sometimes," Lynn said.

"I already told you the story about Shandra, the woman who works at McBurger. That family is now doing well with the moving business," said Lynn.

"That is great. George will appreciate that story. Great adventures. You have one recent recipient, too, you said." Dorothy was eager to hear about another recipient.

"Oh, Mom, this is so sad. I was behind a man, Lucas Hungler, at Harris Teeter. He was putting back groceries because he was short twelve dollars. I pretended to find a twenty-dollar bill on the floor. The cashier and I convinced him to keep it and pay for all his food, which he did. After he left, the cashier told me she went to high school with Sydney, his wife. She just had a baby, but she ended up with an amniotic fluid embolism and is on a ventilator in the hospital. He's struggling to take care of the baby and had to take a leave from work."

"Oh, that's so sad. Were you able to help Sydney in any way?" asked Dorothy.

"Do you remember my friend, Wanda, who now works in maternity?" asked Lynn.

"It's vague. You and George had so many friends; I don't remember them well," said Dorothy.

"I talked to her, and she arranged to have a social worker meet with Lucas. The cashier said she and some of Sydney's friends were willing to help, too, with the baby when the social worker contacted them with Lucas's permission."

"I'll say a prayer for Lucas and Sydney. I'm glad you did what you could for them," said Dorothy.

"That's what I wanted to talk to you about. Did you find there was always more to meeting these people than just giving them the twenty dollars?" asked Lynn.

Dorothy smiled, a knowing smile. "Yes, dear. It's like they become part of the family. It's the involvement I loved. Buying a bike or a different toy was a valuable thing to do, but it lacked contact for me. There was always something these twenty-dollar recipients were struggling with in addition to being able to use the twenty dollars. That's the piece I didn't have the strength to do anymore. I knew you could do that. I thought maybe you would like to do it, too," said Dorothy.

"My mother, the con artist! I'm happy to help anyone I can. Thank you for dinner. Love you, Mom."

Lynn heard her phone beep as she waited for the elevator. It was a text from Wanda.

Sydney had a cardiac arrest. We got her back, but it's not looking good.

This family is going to be a challenging twenty-dollar recipient, Lynn thought. Her heart ached for the family.

40

Dinner with Stan

Lynn got to work early the next day. She had rushed so much getting out of the house that it wasn't until she got to work that she realized she had on one navy and one black Rothy shoe. That had happened once before, from which time Lynn learned to leave an extra matching pair of navy shoes in her office. *We are off to a good start today*, she thought.

She left Wanda s message to call her about Sydney's condition when she had the time and inclination. She wanted so badly to go up to the ICU but restrained herself. Lynn also was sure Wanda would call her. She went on to make her rounds in the ED.

"Good morning, Beatrice. How was the weekend?" Lynn asked.

"Relatively quiet for a weekend; no major car accidents and the potential 'heart attack' turned out to be angina. We do have one growing problem, though," said Beatrice.

"I am waiting to hear. We had five patients with flu symptoms. One was so sick, Dr. Holden admitted him. He's in isolation on the fifth floor," reported Beatrice.

"Thanks for that heads up. I'll check with Doc Holden to see what he wants us to have on hand here. Do you have someone who can check how much personal protective equipment is on hand? We might need to order more," said Lynn.

Back in her office, Lynn called the health department for information about the flu.

"It's going to be a tough one," said Dr. Vincent. This season's influenza B/Victoria viruses are giving us the most trouble. The vaccination rate this year is lower than last year at this time. Not too late for people to get them, either. We are just starting to see the peak, so get ready!"

"I'm on it. We will post our 'get vaccinated' signs and stock up on the meds and PPEs. Keep me posted if things change. We saw five cases last night, so the surge is coming," agreed Lynn.

"You take care of yourself, too," said Dr. Vincent.

Lynn called medical records. "We saw five cases of flu last night. Would you have your IT fellow send us a printout about the number of flu cases seen in the ED, outpatient clinics, and those admitted?" asked Lynn.

"You got it, Lynn," said Martha Jennings.

Once Lynn got the information from Martha, she called the VP of nursing to report the results. The VP of nursing, Claire Rosenthal, scheduled a meeting for all the department heads for the next day. The ED staff put out their posters, promoting vaccinations for flu prevention. There were also handouts in the waiting area about the signs and symptoms of the flu.

Wanda texted her back.

Sydney's holding her own but still unconscious. Getting blood transfusions along with a new anticoagulant. Social worker finding help for Lucas. He comes in and just stands in Sydney's room. Not comfortable talking to her. Hopeful but guarded prognosis.

Lynn texted back

Thanks for the update. Keep me posted. Let me know if I can help!

At five p.m., Lynn headed home to change for her dinner at Stan's house. She was tired but looking forward to seeing him.

Lynn arrived at seven with a bottle of merlot in hand. She dressed in jeans and a v-neck aqua sweater with a single white, pear-shaped freshwater pearl necklace. Her hair was down with gentles swirls at her shoulder.

"Thank you so much," said Stan. "You know you didn't need to bring anything."

"I know, but I wanted to. Wow, something smells good. What are you cooking?" asked Lynn. For maybe the first time, Lynn looked more at Stan, the person versus the cop. He was a big guy, maybe six-four, with broad shoulders and a muscular build. There was a kindness about him that modified any fear generated by his physical appearance.

"It's just spaghetti and meatballs with fresh string beans and a salad. It's my signature dish," replied Stan smiling. "The merlot will be great with it."

"I'm delighted to be here to share your signature dish, neighbor. What fun!" said Lynn.

Stan poured them each a glass of merlot. "Here's to friendly neighbors," he toasted. "Do you want to see the rest of the house?" asked Stan.

"But of course," replied Lynn.

As they toured the house, Lynn began to see yet another side of Stan. The house was more substantial than she had expected, maybe twenty-seven hundred square feet. There were four bedrooms. The large downstairs master bedroom was orderly and understated with just necessities, like lamps and cushioned coasters on the end tables. A few pictures of his two children were scattered around.

The upstairs contained a bedroom for each of Stan's children, Carol and Eddie, and a TV/office room. The bedrooms for the children, while orderly, were delightful. Each included brightly colored bedspreads, teenage electronic gadgets, and walls full of posters of sports figures and current rock bands.

"Where are your kids?" asked Lynn.

"Carol is still away at Vanderbilt, and Eddie is on a school trip to Washington, DC. I got a text from him yesterday, saying he would do the White House tour today. He's so into sports; I'm glad to see him develop some interest in government," said Stan.

"How do you manage your job with your kids? That can't be easy," said Lynn.

"It's simpler now that they can be left alone. Even when Deb is not home, Eddie at sixteen can take care of himself. He's a good kid so far. No worries about drugs or not doing schoolwork."

"I'm sure that's because he's got a good dad," said Lynn.

"Thanks for that. My parents are both still alive. They help out when I'm on a tough case that keeps me away a lot. My mom makes supper for all of us. Thank goodness for them," said Stan.

"I try to help out with my brother's kids once in a while. They still are too young to be by themselves. Love them to pieces," said Lynn." But then I get to go home and leave the primary responsibility to them."

"So, what's next for you? You now have your own house, a great job, and are unattached. What's your new direction?" asked Stan. "I can't imagine you have not given some thought to other life adventures."

"I have given that some thought. Eventually, I'd like to get married and have a family, I guess. I might go back to school for a doctoral-level degree. I'd like to try teaching graduate nursing students. Academia gives me more free time to spend with any kids. But right now, the boxes in my back room are my most pressing concern!" laughed Lynn.

"You know I'm happy to help with your new house anytime, new neighbor."

"I will keep you in mind. Are you up for some work and then a home-cooked dinner?" asked Lynn.

"I'd love it!" said Stan.

"What about you? What are your future life adventures?" asked Lynn.

"I started going to law school, part-time, two years ago. I'm only taking one, sometimes two courses a semester so far. I'd like to do more to help people rather than helping them after trouble has happened to them," said Stan.

"Good for you, Stan. So, tell me about law school." Lynn had to admit she was impressed.

41

Talking with Lucas

LYNN WAS IN HER OFFICE WHEN SHE HEARD A FAMILIAR knock on her door, even though the door was open. She looked up to see Peter in the doorway.

"Enter, good sir. How are you this morning?" asked Lynn.

"I am in excellent spirits. I had this dinner with this lovely woman on Saturday night. It was the best time I've had in ages. If only I knew if she felt the same way."

"Let's see if we can figure that out. Did she smile at you during your date?"

"Oh, yes, and laughed, too."

"Laughing is an excellent sign she was having a good time. Here comes the big test," said Lynn.

"I'm ready," said Peter.

"Did she show signs it was okay to kiss her good night?" asked Lynn.

"Signs? Hmm. I did kiss her good night, and she did not resist. I don't remember any signs, though. What could I have missed?" asked Peter.

"Did she hold your arm and maybe cuddle a little. Did she smile at you on the doorstep?" asked Lynn.

"I think so. I need to pay more attention, though. Darn it!" said Peter.

"I'm quite sure she had a wonderful time. I'm betting it was delightful for her, too."

"Thank you so much. You have made my day. Unfortunately, I'm on call this weekend, but I would love to plan another date. Do you think she would be up for that?" asked Peter.

"I know she would," said Lynn.

"I'll call you," said Peter, all smiles. He got up from his chair and shut Lynn's door. He walked over to her, kissed her lightly on the cheek, and did his usual wave as he walked out the door and back to work.

Lynn saw a text from Wanda.

Lucas is here but ready to go to the cafeteria for coffee. Looks sleep deprived. He visits but doesn't talk to Sydney. Can you speak to him in the cafeteria? Please!

Lynn texted back:

I'm on my way to the cafeteria. Want coffee? One sugar, no cream?

From Wanda:

You are the best and yes, to the coffee.

Lynn got a coffee and a muffin. She looked around for Lucas and found him sitting alone in a small alcove. There was an empty table next to him, toward which Lynn headed.

"Hi," Lynn said after sitting down. "You look familiar. Do I know you?"

Lucas lifted his head and looked at Lynn. "Yeah, you're the twenty-dollar lady in the grocery store, right?"

"Yes, that's where we bumped into each other before. Hope no one here is too sick that you are visiting?"

"I see from your badge that you work here. It's my wife. She's unconscious."

"Yes, I work in the emergency department. I'm sorry to hear about your wife. I hope the docs think she's getting better," replied Lynn.

"They are not sure she'll recover. We just had a baby, too. That's why this happened. I hate the thought of her growing up without her mother and me without my wife. Sydney's such a good person. This should not have happened to her."

"I'm sure your visiting comforts her," said Lynn.

"Everyone says I should talk to her, but she's just lying there not moving. I feel stupid talking to her." Lucas looked so miserable.

"Talking is great. You would be amazed at how much unconscious patients can hear even though they can't move or talk. You want to hear a great story about that?" asked Lynn.

"Sure, why not?" replied Lucas.

"One of our male night nurses took care of this unconscious patient. He would talk to this patient about what car he was looking at to buy. Every night he would speak of seeing or thinking about a different vehicle and the pluses or minuses of buying that car. The patient was unresponsive. The nurse took his two days off and came back to find the patient was awake. The patient recognized the nurse from his voice. You know what the first words were to this nurse?" asked Lynn.

"Thanks for talking to me?" suggested Lucas.

"Close. The patient said, 'What car did you buy?' He also told the nurse he enjoyed hearing about the description of the vehicles from his search." Lynn had Lucas's attention with that anecdote.

"There's been some research on what patients can hear when they appear to be unaware, but this story circulated throughout the hospital. It's one reason the nurses and docs are telling you to talk to your wife," said Lynn.

"So, it can make a difference?" asked Lucas.

"It certainly can, and we know it won't hurt. You could even record your baby's sounds. Give it a try."

"I don't have a recorder," said Lucas.

Lynn took a quick look at Lucas's phone. It was an old and inexpensive phone without recording capabilities.

"Come to my office, and I'll lend you ours. Use it as long as you want," said Lynn.

"Thank you. You made me feel better."

Lynn thought maybe it might be her imagination, but Lucas seemed more hopeful.

Lynn walked to the ED with Lucas and showed him how to use the office's small recorder. They had two of them for forensic interviews when needed. The ED could spare one temporarily.

She was back in the ED in time to help the staff with patients who had suffered burns from a fire at the paper mill. They could treat minor burn wounds, but patients with significant burn wounds would be transported by helicopter to Charlotte's burn unit. Those arrangements fell on her shoulders. She sent a quick text to Wanda:

Talked. Fingers crossed. Burn victims are coming into the ED. Coffee later?

Lynn put her phone in her lab coat pocket before looking at Wanda's next text:

He's talking to his wife—also, new anticoagulants working better.

42

Mom and George

It was now Sunday morning, and Lynn was waiting for George, his family, and Dorothy to come over for brunch. She had invited Peter, but he was on call. He would try to make it if he wasn't involved with patients. *Should she ask Stan*, she had wondered. *We were just friends, right? What's wrong with friends meeting each other? Are they both just friends? Can women have male friends?* Finally, she told herself to stop! She decided she wanted this brunch to be relaxing and did not invite Stan this time.

"Good morning, everyone," Lynn said, opening the door to her family. The kids piled in first, then Angie.

"We came ahead, and George went to pick up your mom. It's a little tight with all of us in one car."

"That's fine. You and I can catch up a little," said Lynn.

"Aunt Lynn, where's the TV and games?" asked Bernie. The two girls stood next to him, nodding their heads.

"Come with me," Lynn said. She took them to the TV room, which Lynn set up with a basket full of toys and a Nintendo game attached to the TV. Eloise and Edison ran to the toy basket and Bernie to the Nintendo.

"Coffee?" Lynn asked Angie.

"Definitely a yes," replied Angie.

"Tough day?" asked Lynn.

"Just busy. I don't know if George mentioned, I've gone back to work."

"No, he didn't say anything about that. Tell me all about what you are doing," said Lynn.

"I am now the vice-principal of Mackinaw High School. I officially start in January but have already been to orientation and other meetings. It's a great job, and I know I'm going to love it. Bernie, Eloise, and Edison are all in school full time this year, and my hours will mostly coincide with theirs," said Angie.

"Wow. I didn't even know you were interested in going back to work," said Lynn.

"I had thought about it. This fall, I wasn't that busy at home with all the kids in school, so I thought maybe I could do some substitute teaching. I love staying home with the kids, but I still want to do something that contributes to the world at large, even if that's only in Deer Park. Mackinaw's principal called me and said their vice principal had resigned because of illness in her family. Would I be interested in that job? George and I talked it over, and he was good with it, except he runs around calling me Pal," said Angie.

Lynn laughed. "I remember when he was so impressed when he learned to distinguish between the words, principle and principal, by thinking of a principal in school as a pal. For some reason, that made a deep impression," laughed Lynn.

"Maybe because when he pulled all those pranks in school, the principal didn't suspend him. Mr. Fargo had a great sense of humor," said Angie.

The doorbell rang. "Come in," said Lynn. "Door's not locked."

"Good morning, my lovely sister. So great of you to invite us. Look that snazzy couch," said George.

Lynn got up to help Dorothy into one of the comfortable chairs. "The couch was delivered on Friday. Thank you very much, kind sir and madam," Lynn said, bowing her head to George and Angie. "I love it."

"Since you love it, I'll take credit," said George. "If you didn't like it, I'd just remind you; you picked it out."

Everyone laughed.

Lynn finished preparing the scrambled eggs, sausages, and toast. There was a large bowl of fruit, juice, coffee, and hot chocolate already on the counter for the buffet. She had set up the table near the window for the seven of them.

"Can I be excused?" asked Bernie after he wolfed down his food. "Sure," said Angie. "Me, too," said Eloise. "And me," added Edison.

"Go, go," said George. "I know you have more exciting things than adult talk in that back room. Your Aunt Lynn was prepared."

"But of course. Stocking the back room with toys for the kids is what aunts and grandmothers do," replied Lynn.

"The plot thickens," said George. "Mom, were you in on this devious plan?"

"But, of course," said Dorothy. "It's important that I stay true to grandmotherhood."

"Now that young prying souls have been removed, we want to hear about your date with Dr. Pete. How did that go?" asked George.

"Talk about prying souls! What did Peter tell you?" asked Lynn. "I know you asked."

"He wouldn't say anything, even when I threatened to post unflattering pictures of him from college on the internet," said George.

"What did he say to that?" asked Angie.

"He just said I wasn't the only one who had unflattering pictures. Sometimes he's too smart for my good," responded George, laughing.

"We had a good time," said Lynn.

"That's it? Aren't you saying anything else? After all my months of matchmaking, that's all I get?"

"I'm just following Dr. Pete's lead. Remember, too, I also have unflattering pictures of you," said Lynn.

"Mom, she's threatening me," said George.

"No sympathy here. You deserve it, and I'm willing to share the pictures I have, too."

"Angie, help me. They are ganging up on me," said George.

"What are you going to do to redeem yourself?" asked Angie.

"I know just the thing. I'll be right back," said George.

The next thing they saw was George coming into the house with two plants for Lynn, the snake plant she had requested, and a red desert rose plant in bloom, showing off its stunning red flowers. The rose plant was similar to the one Dorothy had when Lynn and George were growing up that Lynn loved.

There were tears in Lynn's eyes as she hugged her brother.

43

An invitation from Peter

WHEN LYNN ARRIVED AT HER OFFICE MONDAY MORNING, there were two cups of coffee on her desk. One on her side and the other on the front side of her desk. She pondered this. *Who could have brought in the coffee and left? That's not like Peter to do that.*

"Sorry to invade your space," said Peter. "Beatrice let me in so I could drop off the coffees while I checked on a patient. So how are you this morning?"

"I'm great, thanks. How was your weekend on-call?" asked Lynn.

"A zoo! The holidays make people do dumb things. One fellow was celebrating too much, stepped off the sidewalk knocking over the barriers around a rather large pothole. A fractured ankle, smashed patella, and a broken wrist got him a stay at our lovely hotel."

"The staff said you guys did a great job managing him," said Lynn

"Thank you for that. Speaking of hotels," said Peter, whose voice trailed off a little.

"I'm going to a meeting this weekend about managing an orthopedic service. The speakers will do presentations on financial management, providing care in the ED, on the units, and in ICUs. The conference is in Asheville, with rooms available at the Inn at Biltmore. I would love it if you went with me. Separate rooms, of course! Might be fun?" asked Peter.

Lynn was amazed at how Peter was so confident and on top of work all the time, yet the softer side showed when he asked for a favor. He had this balance between being in charge when he needed to be yet able to ask and negotiate requests with deference.

"Let me check my schedule,' Lynn said as she looked through her calendar. "It says, clean the house this weekend. Yes, I'm free! I would love to go with you and be at the Biltmore at Christmas time. What a treat on both accounts!"

"We should leave on Friday and come back Sunday afternoon. Does that work for you?" asked Peter.

"I can make that work," said Lynn. "Looking forward to this weekend."

"Yeah, me too. Thank you." Lynn got up from behind her desk and walked with Peter to the door. He squeezed her hand and went down the hall to check on one more patient before he left.

Lynn went back to her desk and started on some paperwork. As she drank the coffee Peter had brought, her thoughts drifted to the weekend. She was excited and scared at the same time. It was apparent Peter cared about her and was moving toward a relationship. Everything with Alan had been terrific at the beginning of their relationship, too. It then deteriorated to the point of being intolerable. *How does that happen?* she wondered. She had known Peter much longer than she had known Alan, but it was mostly through work and friendship. George liked him a lot, and it was rare for George to like any of her boyfriends. She believed in the adage; it was easier to get into something than to get out of it. She wished she knew a way to see how this relationship would turn out.

44

Facing fears

At home, worries about the weekend kept creeping into her thoughts. *Would spending the weekend with Peter ruin their friendship? Was she ready for a serious relationship? Would Peter make a good partner? What happened in his marriage?*

Oh, she thought, I can ask George. He would know about that. She could feel the tension in her stomach go down a little.

Too bad I'm not a fortune teller, she thought. Suddenly, she remembered this article she had read in a magazine. It was how a woman figured out how to spot a good versus not so great relationships. She had cut out the story and filed it in her desk drawer.

Perfect for my situation right now, she thought, digging the article out from its file. She poured herself a glass of merlot, snuggled comfortably under a blanket on the couch, and started to read.

Sun in your eyes?

By Allison Jones

I was debating about getting divorced when my husband and I took a mini-vacation to Vermont. I had gotten up early to take my usual morning walk alone. I wasn't happy, but then many people aren't happy. Being un-happy was a feeling that lacked an exact cause. Without that cause, I was stuck. I didn't know if my unhappiness was something fixable or impossible to change.

My husband and I later went for lunch at a restaurant that served food outside on their rooftop. It was a sunny, warm day in July. We were seated at a table with an excellent view of the wooded land. I also had a clear view of an empty table near the entrance to this patio. I watched as a man and woman were seated at the table. The woman was facing the sun, in some distress from the sun's rays. The man offered to switch seats. Now, he was squinting to control the effects of the sun on his eyes. There was a little conversation that I could not hear, but it resulted in them asking the waiter to move them. He honored their request.

I watched another couple be seated at the table. This time the gen-tleman sat with the sun shining on his eyes. The man and woman had a conversation, and they too requested being moved to another table.

I don't remember, at this point, even eating my lunch. I was fascinated by these interactions at this table. Now a third party, again a man and a woman, sat at this table. The woman had the sunny side of the table. She talked to the man, and they switched seats. The man sat squinting. They spoke, and the woman shook her head no. The man continued sitting in the chair with the sun shining brightly in his eyes. The woman seemingly had little concern for his discomfort.

As I thought about it, I recognized my life with my husband was the third scene. I knew my husband would not care if I sat in the seat with the irritating sun. As long as he was comfortable, he was content. If I com-plained and argued about my discomfort in any situation, it would change. However, my husband would not be the one to care about my pain. Unlike the first two couples, I did not have a loving relationship with someone who cared about my needs.

But maybe these two loving couples were a fluke. Was this type of caring within a couple rare?

Later, while visiting a friend in New York City, I went to this indoor mall alone for lunch. The food court was lovely, overlooking the Hudson River with its many ferry boats. I managed to find an empty table near the window. The food was delicious, and the view exceptional. I was ready to leave when I saw this man, maybe in his fifties, looking for a table. I waved him over to let him know I was going.

I mentioned the view from the chair I was sitting in had the best over-look of the water and that he might want to sit on that side of the table. He thanked me for that perspective. He said if that's the seat with the best view, I'll have my wife sit there. As soon as he said these words, I saw his wife coming. I told her what her husband had just said. She smiled and said, "Yes, that's how he is."

After a year of counseling, the therapist asked my husband if he had learned anything from the sessions. All his comments to and about me were negative. After she said that, I realized I either had to accept the situation as it was or leave. It wasn't going to change because that's how he was. I left the marriage. After a few stumbles, I found someone who refuses to let me sit anywhere with the sun in my eyes, actually or metaphorically.

When I have friends who question their relationships, I tell them if you want to know about a relationship, ask yourself, would he or she trade places with you if the sun was shining in your eyes?

The story leads Lynn to think about her relationship with Alan; she remembered a time at one of his real estate occasions. The host had a buffet of rich food, including caviar. She remembered Alan put some of the caviar on the crackers on his plate and insisted that she do the same. Even though she told him she didn't like caviar, he still insisted she eat some to not insult the host. He got angry when she said no.

She doubted Peter would insist she eat caviar after telling him she didn't like it or let her sit with the sun in her eyes. She had thought about this article before. She believed it was more than the act; she had figured that was important. If the gesture came from the heart and not the ego, that's what made the difference. Alan did kind things for her in the presence of others to look good. He occasionally did nice things for her when they were alone, too, but a bouquet usually leads to asking her to do him a favor. But how did one know when a gesture was heartfelt?

45

Lucas and Stan

THE NEXT MORNING AT WORK, LYNN ARRANGED HER SCHED-
ule to be off duty from Friday to Monday. She did not want to chance
not getting back on Sunday. She was drinking her coffee, musing about
the trip when she got a sudden text from Wanda:

**Lucas is heading for the cafeteria. Could use a pep talk—no
change in Sydney's condition.**

The ED was quiet, and under control, so Lynn headed to the cafeteria for coffee and a muffin. Once there, she spotted Lucas in his same
cubby spot. She joined him.

"Good morning," said Lynn. "Do you mind if I join you?"

"Glad to see you. There's no change in Sydney's condition. Nothing
is helping," said Lucas.

"I can only imagine how frustrating this is for you. Are you able to
talk to Sydney? Any recordings?"

"I try talking, but I'm not much of a talker. I'm more of a doer.
I did record the baby and me. I played the recording for her, but she
didn't move or anything."

"What do the doctors say about her condition?"

"She's stable. There's a little improvement with a new drug that they noticed, and she's also not getting worse. I wish I could do more."

"I'm sure your talking to her helps. Do you hold her hand?"

"No, I'm afraid to touch her. She's got so many tubes going into her. I might mess something up."

"When you go back upstairs, ask the nurses to show you how to hold her hand. They will be happy to do that. I have another idea," said Lynn.

"What's your idea? Anything, please," said Lucas.

"How would you feel about leaving the recorder in Sydney's room? The nurses can play it when you are not there. If I remember right, there's a sticker on the back that says the recorder belongs to the ED. It will be safe there."

Lucas got up from his seat. "Thanks!" he said and left.

Lynn stayed a few more minutes, eating her muffin. She needed some downtime, she thought.

She texted Wanda with the plan she had discussed with Lucas. She texted back:

Great plan!

On her way back to her office, she got a text from Stan:

(Stan) Update on Dorika. Cousin filed a suit. Also, the police department updating human trafficking protocols. Could use your input. Can we meet?

(Lynn) Busy with reports right now. Talk over dinner at my house around six-thirty? Got stuff to move around if you are up to it.

(Stan) Perfect. See you then.

Lynn stopped for some crab meat on the way home. She knew Stan liked seafood and steak, of course. Lynn decided to make crab cakes with roasted veggies and brownies with ice cream for dessert. Tasty but simple, she thought. Lynn got home with enough time to change and prepare dinner. Lynn had thoughts about Stan and Peter as she got ready. Being "single" again, she could come and go as she wished without someone putting demands on her time or criticizing her activities. Did she want to give that up so soon?

Stan arrived promptly at six-thirty, carrying a bottle of white wine. Again, she was taken aback a little about how Stan looked different to Lynn. She guessed she saw people differently in their work environment, more in the role they took on. Stan was wearing a blue shirt, opened at the top, tucked into his jeans. Lynn hadn't noticed before how handsome he was. She knew Stan was older than George, so maybe he was in his late thirties to early forties.

"Hi, good to see you. Come on in," said Lynn.

"Hi," Stan said, bending over to kiss Lynn on the cheek. "Wow! The place looks great, plants and everything," said Stan.

"Come on, and I'll take you on tour," Lynn replied. "This is still the disaster area," Lynn said, standing in the back room with the boxes and unplaced furniture."

"This is work central, huh?" asked Stan.

"Yep, the boxes I can manage but the bookcase, I'd like to put in the living room. It's too heavy for me to move."

"How about this? You finish making supper, and I'll move the bookcase. Just show me where you want it," said Stan.

"Don't you need my help?" asked Lynn.

"No, it's not that big. I'll take the shelves off and move it easily."

"Okay, your wine and dinner will be ready!"

When they finished their respective jobs, they sat down to dinner.

"Thank you, kind neighbor," Lynn said, toasting with her wine glass.

"You are so welcome," replied Stan. "And to my lovely neighbor," Stan toasted back. "Dinner looks delicious."

"So, tell me about Dorika and Ambrus's cousin. That poor woman just can't get free from that family," said Lynn.

"The cousin, Bartal, is claiming Dorika and Randy, the superintendent, planned the killing of Ambrus. He is saying Dorika had an affair with Randy before Ambrus died. While it is true, Randy and Dorika are dating now, there is no evidence of them being together before Ambrus died. Bartal says he should get the four hundred thousand dollars in Ambrus's bank account, which he would if Dorika was proven guilty. I don't know if he knows about the $50,000 that was in the apartment.

The detective on the case, with me helping him now, thinks Bartal and Ambrus were working together on something illegal or, at best, unethical. That's how Ambrus got the four hundred and fifty thousand dollars. That's also how Bartal knew about the money since no one told him about it. We're talking to the DA about investigating Bartal to see what kind of illegal stuff he's doing."

"Where does that leave Dorika?" asked Lynn.

"Right now, the DA and the police are playing along with Bartal about his dealings with Ambrus. I can't say a whole lot more, except Dorika is not the focus of any investigation. I think her lawyer knows that, too.

"By the way, these crab cakes are the best I've ever eaten," said Stan, making another toast to Lynn.

"Flattery will get you anywhere," said Lynn. "I do pride myself on making tasty crab cakes. Compliment accepted,"

"Flattery works with you," said Stan. "That's good to know."

Stan and Lynn continued their conversation, including the new human trafficking reporting system with the police department. They also continued their mild flirtations. Stan surprised her with an ardent kiss goodnight as he was leaving. *Uh-oh,* thought Lynn.

46

Mom and the Recipients

It was Thursday morning at the hospital, and Lynn was checking off what she wanted to do before she left for the long weekend. The nurses' work schedule was complete, with that being most important. She was going over the supplies, which looked adequate, with a few exceptions that she ordered.

"Beatrice, you are going to be in charge this weekend while I'm gone. Do you have any questions?"

"I don't think so. I have your phone number on speed dial, so I'm good."

Lynn laughed. "You will be fine. Call me with any questions. I padded the staff a little for the weekend. If anyone calls in sick, you will still have a full complement. I know you will manage very well," said Lynn.

"We all hope you and Dr. Pete have a good time," said Beatrice, smiling.

"This is a very professional conference," replied Lynn.

"That's what I'm telling everyone, too. I've never seen Dr. Pete happier, though. We will miss you guys, but don't you two even think about us."

As Beatrice left, Peter came in with his two cups of coffee.

"Good morning," Peter said, handing Lynn her coffee. "You ready for tomorrow?"

"Almost. I'm just making sure all is in place for Beatrice to run the ED for the long weekend. I'll be ready at noon sharp tomorrow for the pickup," said Lynn.

"I'm doing the same. Paul Fielding is taking over for me while I'm gone. I think I got everything covered. I don't want to be halfway there and then remember something I forgot to do," said Peter.

"Fielding is a good guy. I'm sure he'll do fine, although not as good as you," said Lynn.

"Awe, that's another reason I like you!" said Peter. "Back to the racetrack until tomorrow and the beginning of a mini-vacation with a terrific companion!"

"See you then, with bells on," said Lynn.

Her phone dinged with a message from Wanda:

You need to come up to my office right away!

Uh-oh, thought Lynn. *Something has happened to Sydney.* Lynn didn't text back, she just ran to the elevators as fast as she could.

"What happened?" she asked Wanda.

"Come with me," Wanda said.

Lucas was at Sydney's bedside, holding her hand, playing the recorded sounds of their baby. Sydney was squeezing Lucas's hand, and tears were falling from her eyes. Lucas turned toward them, smiling.

"She's coming back," Wanda said. "We've seen this progression before. It's a great sign."

"You have made my day, Wanda. I'm so happy for everyone. To quote the A-Team, I love it when a plan comes together," said Lynn smiling.

Lynn and Wanda gave each other a high five as they walked down the hall.

Lynn walked back into her office to see a large holiday basket on her desk, full of chocolates and cookies. She read the note.

Hi Lynn:

Here's a token of our appreciation and good fortune to meet you. We can't thank you enough for the twenty dollars toward David's Christmas gift and the great kindness at the hospital when Daniel was in the truck accident, and David fractured his leg. Your presence was the comfort we needed. We hope you have a wonderful holiday!

Theresa, Daniel, and David

She took a picture of the basket to show her mother and then brought the goodies to the nurses' station for the staff. Finally, having finished up her work, Lynn headed to her mother's apartment for dinner.

"Hi, Mom," Lynn said. "How are you?"

"I'm doing quite well, thank you, dear. George is joining us for dessert, too."

"Good to hear. I have news for George that he will like unless he's heard it already."

"Great. I'm looking forward to hearing the news, too."

Lynn poured herself a glass of merlot and sat down with her mother to their maple bacon salmon dinners.

"I have some news for you, too, Mom. Lucas, the fellow I gave the twenty dollars to in the grocery store's wife, is starting to come out of her coma. It looks like she's going to recover. I got a basket of cookies and chocolates from Theresa, who got the twenty dollars in the toy store. Here's the picture."

"That's so nice of Theresa. I'm glad everything is working out for Lucas and Theresa. What about Dorika?" asked Dorothy.

"Dorika's case has another glitch, but according to Stan, should not involve her. The cousin is suing for the money, but the police are looking into his criminal activity."

"There was one more—the gal from McBurgers whose husband got a job with a moving company. How are they?" Dorothy asked.

"Haven't heard from them lately, but I suspect they are doing fine. Mother, this was such a great idea of yours, giving out these twenty-dollar bills. There is one more to give out this holiday season."

There was a knock on the door, and George entered.

"Good to see you, brother dear," said Lynn.

"Two of my favorite women in the entire world," said George, giving Dorothy and Lynn a kiss on the cheek.

"What's for dessert?" George asked. "What's new with you two?"

"We have peach cobbler with vanilla ice cream today," said Dorothy. "It's in that covered dish."

Lynn and George both helped clear the dinner plates and served the cobbler.

"Yum," said George. "Okay, sis, spill the beans now. Dr. Pete has clammed up and is not telling me anything. He said to ask you."

"What's it worth to you, nosey?" teased Lynn.

"You get to eat your cobbler in peace," replied George.

"Okay, okay," said Lynn. "There is an orthopedic conference in Asheville at the Biltmore Estate this weekend that involves equipment purchases and general running of the ortho department. Dr. Pete invited me to go with him—separate rooms."

"Wow! That's impressive, especially at Christmastime. Where are you staying?"

"The Biltmore Inn," Lynn said in a low voice.

"Where? I couldn't hear that," said George and Dorothy at the same time.

"The Biltmore Inn," Lynn repeated.

"Holy shit," said George.

"George, no profanity, please," said Dorothy.

"Mother, your daughter is going away with Dr. Pete for the weekend at the most romantic places in North Carolina," said George. "Shameful."

"Good for her. She works so hard; she deserves a wonderful holiday away. I'm happy for her," said Dorothy.

George took out his cell phone and started texting.

"Who are you texting?" asked Lynn.

"Dr. Pete. I'm telling him to make sure he's bringing enough condoms with him," replied George.

"George!" yelled Lynn and Dorothy.

"Give me that phone," said Lynn, giving George a gentle sock on his arm.

"Mom, Lynn took my phone away," complained George. "She's hitting me, too. I'm just trying to protect her."

"I'm going for my cane to join her," said Dorothy. Laughter ensued.

47

Shandra and Wan

It was the long-awaited Friday morning. Lynn had already packed for the trip. The house was clean, and she had watered the plants.

Lynn was getting ready to leave for her nail spa appointment at Polish Perfect when the doorbell rang. She got to the door soon enough to see the flower delivery truck driving away. A large, brilliant red poinsettia sat at her doorstep, waiting to come in.

Hi Lynn:

Happy holidays to you and your mom!

Thank you for everything, the $20 at McBurger's window, and using us to move you into your new house. Mr. Alan has referred three clients to us already. Business is good!

Hugs,

Shandra, Booker, Darius, and Jasmine

Good to know all four twenty-dollar recipients are doing well, thought Lynn. *Glad to get some rest before the last twenty dollars gets given out.*

There is so much more than giving out money going on, and to think, Mom did this for years.

Lynn arrived at her nine-thirty a.m. nail salon appointment in plenty of time. She could easily be done and back to her house by eleven. When she got back, all she had to do was dress for the trip. Wan would be her manicurist today, someone who had only done Lynn's nails once before. Lynn picked out her light pink fingernail color and her deep red toenail color. She was looking forward to a relaxing hour.

"Good morning," said Wan. "Good day for you?"

"Yes, a perfect day for me. How about you?" asked Lynn.

Wan didn't answer. She had gotten busy getting the water ready for the pedicure. Wan did the usual routine of soaking the feet, trimming the toenails, and applying the polish, with her head down intent on her work. In the meantime, Lynn checked her messages and did some games designed to improve her cognitive status.

How can I get enough pets home to get to level fifteen? she asked herself.

"Everything good here?" asked an older Vietnamese woman.

Lynn looked down at her toes, looking much more attractive in their new, dark red color. For the first time, Wan raised her head. Lynn recognized fear in her eyes.

"Everything is great. Wan is doing a terrific job," Lynn said.

Lynn's feet were now under the feet dryers while Wan worked on her fingernails. There were not many people in the salon yet, but people were sitting nearby. Lynn gauged them to be too close to have a conversation with Wan. She wanted to make sure Wan was okay.

After all her nails were dry, Lynn went to the checkout area. The older Vietnamese woman was doing the money collecting. Lynn used her credit card and gave Wan a twenty percent tip. She wasn't sure Wan would receive much of that tip. She had already decided to provide her with a twenty-dollar bill.

"Wan, can you come here a minute," Lynn said, pointing to a fingernail. Wan looked worried and hurried right over. Lynn watched the older woman go behind the curtain to the back room.

"Everything is okay," Lynn said. "Happy holidays. Call me if you need help."

She slipped the twenty-dollar bill wrapped around her card into Wan's pocket.

"Thank you," whispered Wan.

"See you next time," Lynn said to Wan. Her voice was louder than usual for the shop's matron to hear as she came from behind the curtain. "Good job."

Maybe, I'm just getting paranoid, mused Lynn as she drove home. *It just feels like something is not right in that shop.*

When Lynn got home, she called Stan. He didn't answer his phone, but she left a voicemail:

"Hi Stan, it's Lynn. Will you email me the update on your department's finished policies for trafficked victims when you get a chance? I think maybe I had an encounter with one at the nail salon, Polish Perfect. I'm going to Asheville this weekend for a conference, starting today. Perhaps we can talk when I get back on Monday if you have the time. Have a pleasant weekend."

She was ready for her trip, except for what to wear during the drive to Asheville. She took a quick look at some information Stan had sent her about trafficked victims in a nail salon. There was a police report about a victim in a small town outside of Charlotte.

Police said they opened an aggravated assault investigation involving suspects accused of human trafficking at a luxury nail salon. One victim was forced into involuntary servitude and repeatedly stabbed. The two owners are suspects in the assault of another woman. Police are now asking anyone else who has been a victim of the suspects to come forward.

Lynn was glad she had texted the name of her salon to Stan. She was sure he would have someone check it out. Relieved that helping Wan was in process, she finished getting ready for her weekend away with Dr. Pete.

48

The Weekend with Peter

LYNN WAS STILL DEBATING ABOUT WHAT TO WEAR DURING the drive when a text came through. It was from Peter:

(Peter) I might be a little late. We have a patient with a fractured femur and an MI. Having issues stabilizing him in the ED.

(Lynn) What can I do to help?

(Peter) If you can get an experienced cardiologist here fast, that would be great. The cardiology resident is good but struggling.

(Lynn) I'm on it.

Lynn got her work phone out and called her friend, Dr. Rebecca Moreno.

"This is Dr. Moreno. How can I help you?"

"Hi, Becky. This is Lynn from the ED. We have a critical cardiac/orthopedic patient in the ED with a big fracture and a probable MI. Dr. Pete could use someone with your expertise to stabilize his cardiac condition. There's lunch in it for you if you have the time to come to the ED," said Lynn.

"Since it's you and I'm in the hospital anyway, I'll run down. I'm counting on a tasty lunch or maybe even dinner, my friend," replied Dr. Becky.

"You got it. I'm calling from home. Beatrice is in charge but call me if you need anything above and beyond what she can do. Dr. Pete is there already, with Paul Fielding," said Lynn.

"I'm on my way to the ED. Food needs to include info about you and Dr. Pete, too. The grapevine is buzzing," said Dr. Becky. "I hope the news is good stuff."

"Whatever it takes to get you there," said Lynn, laughing.

Lynn texted Peter:

(Lynn) Dr. Becky is arriving any minute to help out.

(Peter) Bless you!

With Becky and Peter taking care of this patient, Lynn knew he was getting the best care. Becky was a cardiac patient's dream doctor. She went back to deciding what to wear and what else she needed to get done before leaving.

About an hour later, Peter texted her, saying he was on his way to pick her up.

Let the weekend begin, Lynn thought. She was ready.

"Hi," said Peter. He was standing on her porch, grabbing the suitcase and computer bag Lynn had put out earlier. Lynn had not seen him before in casual dress with jeans and a pullover azure blue sweater. She was happy to be his companion. They were on their way when Lynn put the two water bottles she brought into the cup holders.

"Thanks for the water," said Peter. "Didn't even think to do that."

"It sounded like you were a little busy. What happened with your patient?" asked Lynn.

"Good as gold. Becky was a lifesaver. She got his cardiac condition stabilized, so we got him to the OR. He was bleeding, and it had to be quick. Paul will take good care of him. Thanks also for not being upset with the late start."

"Upset? Why would I be upset? You had an urgent situation to manage," said Lynn.

"My ex-wife would have been screaming at me. I understand some of that, too. It's not easy to be married to a doctor. There are a lot of times when emergencies take precedent over family functions," said Peter. It was the first time she had ever heard him talk with regret and sadness in his voice.

"I guess because I have similar pulls on my life, I could empathize. Plus, because I could do a little something, I didn't feel left out but somewhat right in there with you."

"Thank you for that. That's much appreciated. I am thrilled you agreed to come with me to this conference," said Peter.

"I'm happy to be here with you, too. So that you know, my family has a mantra we follow at home and especially on trips," said Lynn.

"Yes, I'm listening,' Peter responded.

"No police, no hospitals, and no IRS. Of course, the IRS isn't too relevant for trips, except for deductions," said Lynn.

"That's rather good. Avoiding anything that would get you into trouble with the police or the IRS or land you in the hospital is an excellent plan to have in mind. I like it. Can I borrow it?" asked Peter. "There are a lot of patients I could say that to."

"So, tell me about this conference," said Lynn. "Also, I've never been to the Biltmore Estate. Tell me about that, too."

For the rest of the drive there, Lynn and Peter talked about the conference, Asheville, and the Biltmore Estate. It was a natural conversation between two long-time friends who liked each other. *Would they still be just friends by the end of the weekend?* She didn't want to lose her friendship.

49

The Weekend at the Biltmore

"OH, MY GOODNESS," SAID LYNN. AS THEY TOOK THE TURN onto the road leading to the Biltmore Estate, she already had the feeling of being somewhere significant. The trail went by a stone wall around an open gate, by miles and miles of trees and open fields used for plantings in the spring.

"I've been here once before but not at Christmastime. That's supposed to be exceptionally grand," replied Peter. "We have tickets, also, to tour the actual Biltmore house."

They pulled up to a staffed entrance gate, where Peter handed out his two tickets. They took the turn up the hill to the Biltmore Inn, where they were staying. It was huge. Several bellmen were standing near the entrance with the luggage carts. They told us we could not use the luggage carts by ourselves. Lynn smiled.

"What's the smile about?" asked Peter.

"I just remembered a trip where George rode on a luggage cart all over a hotel parking lot. They are smart to put the bellmen in charge of them," said Lynn.

Their rooms were almost across the hall from each other. Lynn wasn't sure if she was disappointed or relieved that they weren't adjacent. Her room had a king-size bed with a lovely bouquet of mixed flowers on the desk and a fantastic view of the mountains. Lynn collapsed on the bed to rest for a moment and took in her surroundings.

Because it was late, they decided to eat in The Dining Room, as it was called, in the hotel. From the brochure's description, the Dining Room was one of the one hundred most romantic restaurants in the U.S.

I'm prepared for romantic, Lynn thought. Out of her luggage came her burgundy, v-neck, sleeveless dress, and black heels. She wore her hair down and added her black satin shawl. She was ready.

The knock on the door was from Peter. To say his jaw dropped when he saw her was an understatement.

"You look beautiful," Peter managed to say. They went hand in hand to the restaurant, seated at a window table.

"Thank you for the flowers and the room with the view of the mountains. It is breathtaking," said Lynn.

"Speaking of breathtaking, check out the view of the mountains from here. It's so great to see beauty instead of mangled bodies," said Peter. "Can you see the mountains from your side of the table?"

"I have a peek-a-boo view, but that's okay. I have the mountain view in my room," replied Lynn.

"No, no," Peter said, standing up. "You need to sit on this side," he insisted.

They changed sides, and Lynn smiled again. *That answers that question*, she said to herself. *With Peter, I'd always have the best view and no sun in my eyes.*

"Thank you. It sounds like you needed a break from work," said Lynn.

"I love what I do. I like the surgery as well as the good feeling of helping people function again. It's the pain, suffering, and worry that comes with the work that gets to me sometimes. In some cases, too, there's not a lot I can do for a patient. They might have lived through a terrible accident, but maybe they won't walk again or use an arm. I do need to get away from it now and then. Seeing beauty helps me recharge."

"I get that. However, we may have re-entry issues after this experience," replied Lynn laughing.

"We will just have to plan more of these escapes if that happens," said Peter. "What would you like to drink? A bottle of bubbly? Or your merlot?"

"Bubbly sounds wonderful, but thanks for remembering I like merlot."

Lynn thought how nice it was not to be told how sinful was her preference for merlot. The waiter took their champagne and dinner orders—diver scallops for Lynn and herb-roasted salmon for Peter.

"Do you think it would be awful if I took off my tie? Most of the other guys here don't have one on," asked Peter.

"Comfort is key," said Lynn. "I have a feeling you won't be escorted out if you take off your tie," said Lynn smiling. "Plus, I read in the brochure men are not required to have ties, just collared shirts. But I'm assuming pants, too."

"Okay, I'll leave my pants on," said Peter, laughing.

Peter poured them each a glass of champagne. "Here's to being in a beautiful place with a beautiful woman," said Peter toasting Lynn.

"Thank you! And here's to my handsome, charming companion for the weekend," Lynn toasted back.

Peter nodded in gratitude. "I brought the talk schedules for the next two days," said Peter. He handed Lynn the outline of the talks. "Do you want to go over them?"

"Sure," said Lynn.

"Tomorrow at 9:00 are the Welcome remarks. God bless us; they are only for fifteen minutes," said Peter. "Then, Orthopedic supplies, what do you think?"

"That sounds good for me," said Lynn

"You know I also want your feedback on the talks. You are so smart and good at knowing what's valuable and what is just hype," Peter commented.

Then there's the break, followed by orthopedic supplies in the office. Maybe not of significant interest for you," said Peter.

"I think I'll go to all of them except for the supplies for the doctors' offices. I'd like to tour the Antler Hill Village and the winery during that time. They may have artwork for sale there, too. I'm excited to see the mansion."

"I plan to go to all of the sessions, although sometimes I sneak out if they get dull. After the morning session tomorrow, I can meet you at Antler Hill Village for lunch. Seeing the winery is a great idea. What's this about artwork?" asked Peter.

"I like to collect a piece of art from special places I've visited," explained Lynn. "If I can afford an original painting, I get that. Often, I have to be happy with a lithograph, but that's good, too."

"I have some tools with me. I can chip off a piece of stone from the Biltmore House as a souvenir. What do you think?" asked Peter.

"I understand better now why you and George are such good friends. Remember our family mantra, no police, and no hospitals," laughed Lynn. "I can see the headlines now, 'Renowned orthopedic surgeon jailed for operating on the Biltmore castle."

Both Peter and Lynn laughed so hard that a few heads turned their ways. They ignored them.

"We have tickets to tour the mansion at six p.m. tomorrow. I figured after that we can catch a nice dinner. I can't wait to see how jealous these guys will be when they see you with me," laughed Peter.

"Peter, I haven't seen this side of you before. You are never competitive at work." Lynn felt a red flag had just fallen on the floor. Was she the trophy date for Peter?

"Wait until you meet some of these guys. They are wolves. You be careful," replied Peter.

"Here's my deal. I may dance with a few guests at a party, but I always go home with the man who brought me," said Lynn.

"Okay, that's some reassurance," said Peter smiling.

"So, tell me what antics you and George pull together. I need blackmail information for when he gets out of hand," said Lynn.

It was pleasant, thought Lynn, listening to Peter tell stories about him and George in college. She felt a connection to Peter, more profound than she had ever felt with a man before. It was easy, too, like being in love with your best friend. She felt happy yet nervous at the same time. When they kissed goodnight before going into their separate rooms, Lynn felt a loss of control. She didn't know if she could keep fighting the feelings she had for Peter. *Don't fall for Peter, yet. It's too soon*, she kept saying to herself.

50
Stan

Stan was up early that Saturday morning. His pancake mix and fruit bowl were ready for breakfast. He had taken his biscuits out of the oven and was getting the bacon prepared to fry. Now all I need is the kids to wake up, he thought, when Carol appeared in the kitchen.

"Good morning, Dad," Carol said. "You are in a great mood this morning. I heard you whistling earlier."

"My daughter's home from college. What could be better?" Stan replied.

"Don't give me that, although it's nice to hear you are happy to have me home. You seem happier, in general. So, what's going on? Did you get a promotion? Are you dating?" asked Carol with great enthusiasm.

"Can't a fellow just fix breakfast for his family without getting interrogated?" replied Stan.

"Something is up. I can feel it," said Carol.

"What's up besides pancakes and bacon?" said Eddie walking into the kitchen.

"Dad's particularly happy this morning. I think he's got a girl-friend," said Carol.

"Dad, is that true? Have you been holding out on me?" asked Eddie.

"I exercise my right not to incriminate myself," replied Stan. "Let's eat."

"You see how happy he is. You see how evasive he's being. Something is up," said Carol.

"Give the guy a break, will you, Matlock. He's happy because I'm here ready to dive into those pancakes and the rest of the food," said Eddie.

"You and your stomach! I'm not giving this up, though. I'll find out before the day is over. Speaking of which, is today Christmas shopping day? Are we getting a tree?" asked Carol.

"Yes, yes, and yes. Now eat and get dressed. We have a lot to do today," replied Stan.

They all sat down to eat together for the first time in a while.

"So, tell me about school, Carol. How was your first semester now that it's over?" asked Stan.

"I loved it! Classes are great, as are my classmates. It's so intellectually stimulating," responding Carol.

"Oh, great, that's what I have to look forward to," replied Eddie. "What about the football team? Did you go to any games? You need to get a life, intellectually stimulating indeed."

"Those knuckleheads! Are you kidding me? I wouldn't be caught dead at one of those games," said Carol.

"Eddie has a point," said Stan. "Maybe he and I could come up to the school and go to a game. You can come to the game if you want or just visit with us. I'd even take you out to a nice restaurant," added Stan to the discussion. In the back of his mind, he thought maybe Lynn would like to go.

As they chattered, Stan felt how good it was to have both kids home. They were his life, but they were growing up. Soon Eddie would be going to college. He knew Carol was right that he was incredibly happy. She wasn't aware it was because of his dinner with Lynn. He was hoping that the relationship would grow. It felt so good to be at her house moving furniture and eating a home-cooked meal. He missed that. He was debating about buying Lynn a present for Christmas, too.

He reread the text Lynn had sent him about a possible trafficked victim encounter. *She had said she was going to be at a conference in Asheville. I wonder what conference that was and with whom she went. Tonight, after shopping with the kids, I'll check out meetings this weekend in Asheville,* he thought.

Shopping had been fun and a great success. Now it was time for the tree. Carol and Eddie ran around the tree lot, looking for the best one. Last year, they came upon an eight-footer, which barely made it through the door.

"Dad, Dad, we found one," they said in unison.

"Okay, okay, I'm coming," Stan replied. He had to admit they found an imposing-looking balsam fir. "This type of tree needs daily watering. Who is volunteering to do that?" he asked?

"I will, I will," said Carol.

"Me, too," said Eddie.

"Okay, it's a deal. We'll get the tree in the stand tonight and decorate it tomorrow. Sound good?" asked Stan.

After the tree was in place but yet to be decorated, Stan went to check conferences in Asheville going on this weekend. He found a meeting on leading a faith community, one for charity organizations, an orthopedic conference, and a recovery conference on substance abuse, mental health, trafficking and abuse, human services, and other healthcare issues. He assumed the recovery conference would interest Lynn.

51

Peter and the Conference

BOTH LYNN AND PETER WERE UP EARLY THE NEXT DAY FOR breakfast and the first conference talk. The meeting was scheduled to be held in the Vanderbilt Ballroom at their hotel, a room almost as large as Lynn's new house. The first talk was about orthopedic supplies in hospitals. The next one was about orthopedic supplies in the office, which Lynn had decided not to attend.

"How did you sleep?" Peter asked Lynn over breakfast.

"Great. I was out as soon as my head hit the pillow. When I woke up, though, I immediately looked at the clock to see if I was going to be late for work," Lynn replied and laughed. "How about you?"

"Same here, except for the work part," said Peter. "I guess I needed a break from the hospital more than I realized. I'm hoping we can escape together more often. I'm happy you came."

"Me, too," said Lynn. She was about to tell Peter she needed to take this relationship a little slower when they announced it was time for the first session on supplies.

"Wow, that was helpful," said Lynn, as they were leaving the first session. "Impressive talk. We should go over what you need in the ED in addition to what's already there."

"Hi, Peter, how is it going with you? Good to see you, man. Who is this lovely creature with you? Wow!" said a man whose name tag read Archie.

"Lynn, this wolf in doctor clothes is Archie Brown. He and I did our orthopedic residencies together. Watch out for him," said Peter.

"Now, now. You know I'm harmless. Besides which, you owe me big time, Peter," said Archie.

"What? I don't remember you doing something special for me. Since we were both poor as the proverbial church mice, I know I didn't borrow money," replied Peter.

"Ah, how soon we forget. I let Peter beat me out of the chief resident position our last year at Emory," said Archie, taking Lynn's arm and tucking it under his extended elbow. "I'm going to have coffee with your girlfriend now and will hopefully convince her to have dinner with me sometime."

Peter somehow managed to get between Archie and Lynn. "No, you don't, Mr. Wolf. You see that gorgeous woman over there in the fourth row. She's been checking you out. I'll bet she would love to have coffee with you."

"The redhead or the blonde?" asked Archie.

"Both, I think," said Peter.

Archie turned to Lynn. "So sorry, my lovely, but duty calls to help as many women as possible." He bent down and kissed Lynn's hand. "If you ever get tired of old Peter here, call me." With that, he slipped Lynn his business card and left.

"What was that?" asked Lynn.

"That, my dear, was what I meant about some of the docs here being wolves. There's something about being at these conventions that makes them a little crazy! Archie, with all his talk, is harmless. He'll be in bed watching TV as soon as dinner is over. That was more to pull my chain a little. Not that he wouldn't have loved to go with you for coffee, lunch, or dinner."

"Wow. I've never had a doctor approach me like that, although I did have one resident who used to follow me into a huge walk-in linen supply closet. Is it safe for me to go to the Antler Hill Village without you?" asked Lynn. "I didn't bring my pepper spray."

"It's always better to be with me," said Peter, "but I think you will be fine. I'd love to hear more about this linen closet resident. I'll meet you at the winery at noon. We can grab a quick lunch at the Village before we head back for the talks.

"It's a deal," smiled Lynn.

Peter squeezed her hand, and they both went their separate ways. Lynn found out she could walk to the Antler Hill Village from the hotel. She came across the winery first and walked through the tunnel that leads to the store. It was covered in Christmas lights as far down the walkway as she could see. *Wow!* she said to herself. Along the way were pictures and stories about the creation of the winery. The store was equally impressive with bottles of Biltmore wine and appealing stations of kitchen and wine paraphernalia.

Leaving the other entrance to the winery, Lynn found herself in the middle of the Village's lower end. She felt like she had entered a Christmas wonderland. Trees decorated with lights and ornaments filled the square. Gorgeous poinsettias were everywhere. She saw a sign for *Cedric's Tavern* and made a reservation there for lunch. In one enclosed area, she watched the multiple antique-looking trains run around between trees, over terraces, poking in and out of tunnels behind replicated train stations and past replicas of the Eiffel Tower and London's Tower Bridge.

George's kids would love seeing this, thought Lynn. *I wonder if Peter likes trains.*

Speaking of which, she saw Peter walking around outside. She called to him.

"Trains! Peter said. "I love trains. Played with them for hours when I was a kid."

He was so joyful. "It's great seeing you so happy," said Lynn.

"I am happy. I love being with you in such a romantic place," said Peter. He kissed Lynn, rather passionately, in the middle of the train exhibit. Some of the visitors cheered and clapped.

Cedric's Tavern was another experience of exceptional furnishings with total comfort and terrific service.

"What are you having?" asked Peter.

"I think I'm going for the fish and chips," said Lynn.

"Me, too," said Peter.

52

Tour of the Biltmore House

THE AFTERNOON CONSISTED OF A TALK ON CONTROLLING INfections and new wound treatments.

"I thought the talks were good, except we already do most of what Dr. Riley said about wound treatments. I was hoping for more," said Lynn.

"That's because I make the residents read all the latest treatment options and report them every month. We try to keep up," said Peter.

"I guess you do. Remind me to never have a water glass near me if I'm invited to speak somewhere," said Lynn.

"I think Riley knocking over his water glass onto his notes, and most of the table, was just a ploy to wake us all up," said Peter laughing.

"Are we going to the cocktail hour?" asked Lynn.

"Ordinarily yes, even with all those wolves around. We just won't have time. It will take us close to thirty minutes to drive to the Biltmore House for the tour," said Peter.

They drove by the multiple fields that in warmer weather boasted of grapevines, vegetable crops, and flower gardens.

"The brochure says the Vanderbilts believed in growing their food for their family and guests. Farm-to-table is the term they used. Besides the crops, they now also have grazing livestock, Angus beef, pigs, and poultry. It's a working farm," said Lynn.

"Sounds like you know a little about farming," said Peter.

"Yep. My grandparents grew many of their vegetables and had chickens. When I stayed over there, I often was sent to get eggs out of the coop. I carried a big stick to fend off the rooster. It turned out to be an excellent experience when I started dating," said Lynn.

Peter laughed as they pulled into the parking lot down from the Biltmore House. They walked the forest path to the stairs that led across the enormous lawn to the house. To say the place was incredible from the view from the top of the stairs was a gross understatement.

The tour started at the entrance hall and proceeded through huge rooms, labeled mostly by their activities, such as the billiard room, breakfast room, which incidentally contained two Renoir paintings, dining room, and Lynn's favorite, the library. The two-story library had ten thousand volumes in eight languages. Lynn could see herself reading in one of the cozy chairs. The bedroom suites were upstairs, exceptionally well preserved with silk damask draperies, paintings, and oak-paneled sitting rooms. The spiral staircase rises four floors with a hundred and two steps. Lynn and Peter climbed them all before they headed back to the dining room in the hotel.

"What would you like to drink, my lady?" asked Peter.

"I think a glass of merlot from the Biltmore winery would be outstanding," said Lynn with a slight aristocratic air.

"Perfect," said Peter replicating her aristocratic air.

Both again ordered the soup, with Lynn selecting the salmon and Peter the lamb rack.

"So how was your day, my dear?" asked Peter.

"Enchanting and productive," said Lynn.

"Tell me about the enchanting part," said Peter.

"But first, you need to tell me how your day was," said Lynn.

"Full of happiness," said Peter. "Being here with you created the best day I've had in years."

When dinner was over, they walked back to the rooms, hand in hand.

"Would you like to come in for a nightcap?" asked Lynn. "I brought some double chocolate liqueur in the little bottles. Sometimes I like it as a nightcap."

"But of course," said Peter.

Lynn poured them both a glass of liqueur and handed one to Peter. He took a sip but then placed the glass down on the coffee table.

"I am so happy to be with you," Peter said, holding both her hands. "You are now the first person I want to see in the morning at work. I think about you all the time. I'd follow you into a linen closet any chance I had," Peter said, smiling and pulling Lynn toward him.

"I'm getting spoiled with the morning coffee you bring and you visiting each morning. My heart feels missing because you have stolen it. I tried to fight how I feel about you, Peter, but it's hopeless," replied Lynn.

Peter took Lynn in his arms and kissed her. For both of them, it felt like they had shut out the world and entered a blissful state of togetherness.

53

Lynn and Stan

AFTER THE SUNDAY MORNING TALKS, LYNN AND PETER grabbed lunch at a restaurant in Antler Hill Village and then headed back home. The ride back was different. They had driven to the conference as friends but were going back more like a couple. They were happy and chatty, but both knew there were some hurdles to overcome before becoming more committed to each other. Neither wanted to discuss those hurdles on the ride back, preferring to stay in the warmth and connection between them.

Lynn arrived at work on Monday morning. She caught up with Beatrice.

"OMG, it was a crazy weekend," said Beatrice.

If she only knew how great my weekend was, thought Lynn. *Concentrate, you are at work, she told herself.*

Beatrice pulled out her list of patients. "In the three days you were off, we had ten patients come in with chest pain, three patients who had attempted suicide, five patients from a multiple car pileup, plus twenty-two patients with flu symptoms. The flu is spreading with people getting together because of the holidays," Beatrice reported. "Somehow, we managed to assess and treat them all. The docs admitted three patients to the medical ICU, two to the surgical ICU, five to various hospital units, and discharged thirty to home."

"Good job, Beatrice. I'll add this report to your performance evaluation. You are off for the next two days. Get some good rest—you deserve it," replied Lynn.

Lynn made her to-do list. She decided to see if Wan Nguyen had been seen in the ED as a priority. She pulled up her name and read through her three admissions.

September 9 - Severe headache—bruises noted on her left arm

October 21 - One attempted suicide—unrelated older female provided constant surveillance; patient talked little; suspicious bruises; older woman refused psychiatric follow-up for the patient.

November 30 - Urinary tract infection—patient, when alone, said she could not go to the bathroom when she needed to—told to hold it in.

Lynn thought the admissions pointed to a severe stress response. Although she couldn't rule out sex trafficking, it was more likely to be labor trafficking. She knew from working with Stan before; labor trafficking fell into a different category of human trafficking. It was involuntary servitude to do work but not sex, although sometimes both happened. It still involved fraud or coercion. The traffickers forced their victims to work with no pay and confined them in some form of substandard housing when not working.

Lynn called Stan.

"Hi, Stan," said Lynn. "Based on her visits to our ED, I do think someone at the nail salon is forcing the woman I saw to work there. Can we meet?" asked Lynn.

Stan was delighted to hear from Lynn. "How about lunch or dinner?" Stan replied. "Glad to meet up with you."

"Today is my first day back from the long weekend, so dinner would be easier for me if that works for you," replied Lynn. "Something casual and quick would be good. I have a feeling I'm going to be wiped out by the end of the day."

"How about the *Diner* at six o'clock? Does that work for you?" asked Stan.

"Perfect. I'll meet you there."

Lynn looked at her schedule for the day. She had a director's meeting at ten with the VP of nursing and a staff meeting at two with her staff. In between, Lynn needed to check the supplies that need replacing and go over the week's staffing schedule. She needed coffee!

"Good morning, sweetie," said Peter, holding two cups of coffee.

"You are such a lifesaver," said Lynn. "Plus, it's good to see you."

"Tough morning?" asked Peter.

"Not too bad, just a lot of catching up, plus meetings," said Lynn. "How's your day going?"

"There were a few screw-ups and some ruffled feathers with the OR staff. I'm going to spend a lot of my day apologizing and getting our service's smooth flow back on track. Nothing too horrible. However, I keep wishing we were back at the Biltmore. That's making it hard to focus," said Peter.

"I have that same problem. How can we fix our desires for some more fun times?" asked Lynn.

"Dinner with me tonight?" asked Peter.

"I wish I could. I'm meeting with Stan, our police liaison, at the Diner over dinner about a potential trafficking victim. I know you are on call tomorrow. How about Wednesday or Thursday?"

"He is a lucky person. Thursday is great. How about you come to my house? Seven o'clock? You can meet my daughter, Hanna, too. She's with me for the week."

"I'd love that." Lynn got up to walk Peter to the door.

"I want to kiss you, you know," Peter said.

"And I want you to, but I don't want to feed the rumor mill which already has our names running through it. I'll take a rain check for Thursday," said Lynn.

"I guess I can live with that promise until then," Peter said. His tone was dramatic, and he had his head down sorrowfully as he left.

Lynn was now smiling and upbeat, ready to face the rest of the day. She just loved Peter's sense of humor.

54

Dinner with Stan

Stan was at the diner when Lynn arrived. He started to get up from his seat, but Lynn signaled him to stay seated.

"Good to see you," said Stan. "Hope you had a good weekend."

"It was great. Asheville is such a cool place. I even got a chance to tour the Biltmore Estates. I was never there before," replied Lynn.

"My wife and I had toured the Biltmore. Isn't it spectacular at Christmastime?" A small amount of sadness had crept into Stan's voice.

"I'm sorry she's gone," said Lynn. "It must be hard on you and the kids."

"Christmas is a particularly tough time, although we are doing better. We went shopping for presents yesterday and even got a live tree. The first one since Wendy died."

"That's great. Good for you guys. Re-establishing old positive events is so important. My mother did that after my step-father died," said Lynn. "Let me tell you about this possible trafficking victim. I have a small issue with confidentiality. I call tell you everything that happened at the nail salon without a problem. I can't share info about her admissions until it becomes a police case."

"Tell me what you saw; then I can fill you in on implementing the new trafficking policies with this case," suggested Stan.

"I went to get a mani-pedi at the nail salon on Friday morning."

"Before you go any further, what in the world is a mani-pedi? It sounds obscene?" asked Stan.

"It's short for manicure and pedicure. Not obscene at all!" said Lynn laughing. A bright smile lit up Stan's face, too. Lynn noticed what an attractive smile he had.

"The woman who did my mani-pedi looked to be in her late teens at the most. Her name is Wan Nguyen. I noticed that she barely talked, and when she did, her head was down, speaking in barely a whisper. The older woman who runs the shop was hovering. She also is the only one who takes the payments. She has eagle eyes on everyone. When she went into the back room, out of sight, I slipped Wan a twenty-dollar bill wrapped around my business card. Wan looks scared all the time and is as thin as a rail."

"I trust your instincts, but that's not much to go on. We do have a woman who goes undercover in nail salons. I don't know for sure if she gets mani-pedis," said Stan smiling again."

"I can tell you, Wan looked stressed, and her ED admissions indicate severe stress. Something bad is happening to this young girl."

"Did she say anything else that might be helpful?" asked Stan.

"Now that I think of it, she did say she was sad because everyone is seeing their family over the holiday, but she's not allowed to see hers. I do remember thinking that it was strange that someone could 'not allow' her to visit with her family. If she had said she couldn't afford to see them, that would have been different."

"That's perfect. It suggests a restriction of Wan's freedom of movement. That means I can send Molly Peterson undercover at the salon. Molly has a knack for engaging victims. Good work, to you, too, Lynn," said Stan. "That fits nicely into our new guidelines. We get a lot of referrals about potential trafficked victims from community members, particularly human service agencies. In many ways, they are similar to what you noticed. We just needed better guidelines to decide if this was a case worth investigating."

"That makes sense. The police could be wasting a lot of time investigating false leads," said Lynn.

"Exactly. The guidelines we have to go out on cases now must have one of five characteristics: there are complaints by the victim of a restriction of movement like Wan said; claims of bondage to pay off a debt; signs of forced labor or sex; vestiges of slave-like practices; or physical abuse. So far, these guidelines show about eighty percent of the victims we do see are trafficked or suffering from abuse. We are still evaluating the impact of using these guidelines."

"Wow, that's impressive. I'm assuming that information would be helpful for my staff. They could ask seemingly innocent questions about those types of features in the complaints of the patients. Are you available to give the nurses and maybe some of the docs a talk?" asked Lynn with some pleading in her voice.

"Sure, I'd be delighted. Just let me know where or when. In the meantime, though, I'll start working on Wan's situation. Molly is exceptionally good at her job."

"We will be in touch then. Sounds like a plan," said Lynn, pleased with this meeting. She couldn't help but wonder if Stan thought something beyond friendship could develop between them.

"My pleasure," said Stan. "Always good to be with you." He hugged Lynn right before they parted in different directions towards their cars.

Back at home, Lynn started thinking about Peter and Stan. She believed both of them would be good to her in a serious relationship. Lynn wished she knew more about their married lives. What made their wives happy or miserable? How could she find out, she wondered?

Lynn got a text from George.

I can't wait to hear about the weekend! Kids want to know if you can come over tomorrow and read them at least part of the paper star story. They insist only you read that story like it's supposed to be read. We will feed you after the reading!

Lynn agreed.

55

The paper star story

AFTER WORK THE NEXT DAY, LYNN WALKED INTO GEORGE'S house, immediately greeted by three enthusiastic children.

"Aunt Lynn, Aunt Lynn, would you read us the paper star story? Pleeeeease! Pleeeeease," said Bernie. Both George and Angie nodded their heads, indicating their approval.

"All right," said Lynn. "But only half the story today. We'll save the ending closer to Christmas, agreed?" asked Lynn.

"Yes, Aunt Lynn. Can we all climb on the bed you used to sleep in?" asked Eloise.

"Sure," said Lynn.

There was a mad scramble to her former bed. *The Paper Star* book was in her purse. Lynn began reading.

"The Paper Star"

By Lorraine Madison

"Man, I hate seeing my name on that paper star dangling from that tree! It's like the whole world knows we are poor now," said Tyler Baranowski to his best friend Tommy Gamble as they strolled the mall.

Tyler's mom and dad had sat down with Tyler and his two brothers to tell them what to expect this Christmas. "You know I'm trying to find work, but the work's not there. We have to spend what little money we have on the mortgage, food, and clothes," Martin Baranowski said. "We can't afford much for Christmas presents this year, so your mother and I submitted your names to United Support. They put your first name on a paper star on the tree in the middle of Somerset Mall with a list of five things you want for Christmas. Someone in town takes your star and buys you a minimum of three of the items you've put on the list," his father explained.

"Look at it this way, my name's on that tree every year," said Tommy. "This is the first for you. You think it's bad that people know you're poor and taking charity—wait until you see what you do or don't get for Christmas from the people who pick your name! It can be downright awful!"

Tommy and Tyler reached the food court and settled in on one of the tables to split a soda.

"Do you remember the green coat I wore all last year?" asked Tommy.

Tyler laughed. "The one we use to call you pea pod when you wore it. Man, that was the worst color green I'd ever seen in my life. Your mom must have been smoking something when she picked that out."

"My mom didn't pick that out. Someone who got my name off the tree bought it. I had to wear it because it was the only coat I had."

"Oh, brother. You mean I could get a coat like that this year? I'd burn it first and go cold," said a determined Tyler.

"I don't want a green coat," interrupted Eloise.

"It's okay, sweetie, you won't be getting one," Lynn told her.

"Don't interrupt," said big brother Bernie. "Keep going, Aunt Lynn.

"No, you wouldn't burn the coat. Your mom would say wearing an ugly green coat is better than freezing as my mom did. You'd wear it, and everyone would laugh." Tommy fought back the watery feeling in his eyes.

"This just gets worse and worse," said Tyler. "What else could someone buy that would disgrace me?"

"Tell me what you put on your list, and I'll give you the bad news," said Tommy.

Tyler was beginning to be worried. Having his name on the tree was bad enough, but then getting awful stuff he'd have to wear or use, well, then he might have to go live with a relative out of town.

"I put I wanted a bike, a baseball glove, and then my mom made me add some clothes, like pants, a shirt, shoes, and a coat." Tyler paused. "Oh, no, I have a coat on my list."

"Chances are you won't get the bike. It's too expensive. There you might be lucky. Otherwise, you could get a pink girl's bike. Your mom and dad would make you ride it."

"No way! You mean these people who pick up these stars don't look at the names to see if it's a boy or a girl?"

"You know my brother, Les? It's bad enough that his real name is Leslie. He's always getting into fights because of that. Somebody didn't look where it said Leslie was a boy and bought him all girl stuff, including a pink bike! He painted over the pink and made it black. Unfortunately, he couldn't do anything with the girl bar that went down instead of straight across. But that's not the worst that can happen," continued Tommy.

"What could be worse than getting a pink girl's bike for Christmas when you're a boy?" Tyler had this vision of himself riding a pink girl's bike wearing an ugly green coat.

"Two years ago, my brother's name, my sister's name, and mine were taken off the tree. The person who took my little sister's name never bought her a thing. Les and I got a lot of what we asked for, and it was decent stuff. Melanie got nothing—she was five at the time. Before Christmas, my mom knew that Melanie's person hadn't gotten her anything, so she went to

Goodwill and picked up a few things for her. Sadly, she couldn't afford the new doll Melanie wanted."

"Man, oh man, I thought it was bad we were eating so much spaghetti."

When Tyler got home, he slunk into the chair in front of the television. Usually, he'd check to see if his brothers wanted to do something but not today.

"Tyler is that you with the TV on?" said his mother from the kitchen. "Come here and see if these cookies taste any good."

He'd been so down about Christmas; Tyler hadn't noticed the smell of his mom's cookies permeating the house. He enthusiastically grabbed a cooled chocolate chip cookie from the plate on the table. "I don't know, Mom. I think I have to try another one to see if they are good or not."

His mother laughed. "Okay, but only one more. I don't want you spoiling your dinner." After a brief pause, she said, "So what's with the TV after school? That's not like you."

"Tommy told me I might get an awful green coat and a pink girl's bike from that star thing. We shouldn't have done that, Mom."

"Wow, wait a minute. What's this about the green coat and a pink bike?"

"Tommy said that's what happened to him and his brother. AND, one year, his sister was supposed to get some presents but didn't. The person who took her name forgot her. That could happen to us, too."

"I admit, it could happen," said Tyler's mom, now sitting next to him. "I think you and Tommy are missing the point about this Christmas star. There are good people in this town, strangers, willing to help out, and make your Christmas better. Sometimes people make mistakes. Sometimes people can't help out, even if they have promised, because something has happened to them. That's life, son."

"But Mom, if I don't get a good bike, I can't get around. Suppose the person who took my name doesn't get me a bike?"

"A bike is a big present to ask for from a stranger. You might not get a bike for Christmas. If you don't get a bike, your dad and I will figure out how to get you a good used one. Remember, Tyler, the person who took your name wants to help. It would be best if you were grateful for his or her kindness. You'll meet people who help you along the way because they are good people. They may not always help exactly the way you want, but they try. Then others don't care. People who take those stars off the tree are caring people. You need to be appreciative of whatever they give you for Christmas."

"But Mom!"

"No buts. If you don't want to play with your brothers, then it's home-work time. No TV until after you do your homework! You know better than that."

During the next few weeks, Tommy and Tyler checked the tree to see if anyone had picked the stars with their names on it. Tommy's name went first. Soon Tyler's star and those of his brothers disappeared from the tree. All the names from Tommy's family were gone, too. The tree looked bear with only a few stars left dangling.

In the meantime, Tyler's bike was falling apart. The tires were going flat all the time. He worried the brakes weren't going to hold much longer. Pretty soon, he would have to junk this old bike. It had served him and his brothers well, but as Tommy said, "It's terminal."

Tommy continued to regale him with other horrible Christmas present stories. There was a glimmer of hope when Tommy did confess, he'd gotten his BMX bike for Christmas from someone who had picked his name.

"So, it's possible to get a decent bike for Christmas?" he asked.

"Possible, but not likely," said Tommy, now the sixth-grade authority on what you can expect for Christmas from various local charities. The town's unemployment rate was eleven percent. More boys and girls than ever had their names submitted to local charities for the first time. Kids *who ignored and ridiculed Tommy before now invited him for sodas to talk about what to expect on Christmas. Tommy's prophecies of a doomsday Christmas, with only a flicker of hope, spread rapidly throughout his class.*

The only person who remained hopeful was Tyler's mother. As the days before Christmas got crossed off the calendar and only a week remained, she was even more optimistic. "Tyler, you're worrying too much," she said. "Everything will work out, you'll see. Remember, though, all these people who pick up the stars are trying to do good. Be appreciative."

Is Tyler going to get a pink girl's bike for Christmas?" asked Eloise. Lynn had closed the book.

"We will have to see what does happen to Tyler," said Lynn. "To be continued."

"Thank you, Aunt Lynn," said Bernie. "It was nice of you to read that part of the story."

"Thank you for being appreciative," said Lynn smiling.

Lynn grabbed a bite to eat with Angie and George. It was getting late, so George agreed to wait until tomorrow when he and Lynn were at Dorothy's to talk about the weekend.

56

Mom and George

AFTER WORK THE NEXT DAY, LYNN DROVE TO HER MOTHER'S house and saw George waiting for Dorothy's floor elevator.

"So, you were able to make it here," said Lynn, poking her brother in the ribs, just for fun. She was in a good mood.

"She was my mother first, you know. Just because you were cute and adorable doesn't mean you still get all the attention," replied George.

"No, I know you are here for some other reason, too," Lynn said.

"Hi, Mom," George said. "Lynn said I didn't deserve to be here for dinner."

"No, I didn't. I just know George has got an ulterior motive for being here, but he won't tell me what it is," said Lynn.

"I'm surprised, Lynn, you didn't suspect right away he wants to know about your weekend with Peter," said Dorothy.

"I can tell you it was terrible. Peter and I argued all the time; the hotel was disgusting, as was the food and the Biltmore House," said Lynn.

"I am crestfallen," said George. He hung his head down and puckered his lower lip.

"You were hoping for something different?" asked Lynn.

"Yes, I expected the TRUTH," said George.

"I don't think you can handle the truth," said Lynn laughing.

"Okay, you two. That's enough. George, that's too much poking around in your sister's personal life. Lynn, don't lie, just tell him to bud out," said Dorothy.

"Okay, Mom," Lynn and George said in unison, laughing.

"So, did you have a nice time, dear?" asked Dorothy.

"Yes, I did, but I have some questions. I know Peter from work and now a little more about him personally. He's competent, compassionate, well respected, and one of the best docs with whom I work. He could be different in personal relationships," said Lynn. "I've experienced that before. So, what's he like away from work?"

"I remember Peter coming over to the house with George when he was in high school and college. He was always polite and respectful. I remember thinking Peter was smart with a good head on his shoulders and had a playful side. That's probably why he and George got along so well. I liked George spending time with him, rather than Louis Durango."

"Now, wait a minute. Louis was a great guy. He even had a good weed source," said George.

"Don't worry, Mom. George never smoked the stuff. I remember that," said Lynn. "He's just teasing you."

There was a knock on the door. George let the server bring in dinner, which tonight consisted of stuffed flounder, red rice, and asparagus with gingerbread for dessert.

"So, what is your worry about Peter?" asked George as they sat down to eat. He looked at his sister as if he could figure out what was troubling her.

"We all know at the beginning of a relationship; everyone puts their best foot forward. We all have our faults and quirks. We don't find them out until later, often after committing ourselves to the relationship," said Lynn.

"Except for me, since I'm as close to perfect as they come," said George.

"But of course, dear," said Dorothy.

"Mom always was supportive of your delusions," said Lynn.

"I'll ignore that. I'm guessing you want to know about any faults and quirks that Peter has. Right?" asked George.

"I would say the main issue his ex-wife, Virginia, had with him was the amount of time he spent at work. From what she has said, she thought once his residency was over, he'd have more time to spend with her and their daughter. That didn't seem to happen to her satisfaction."

"Being a doctor isn't an easy life for the family. I've answered plenty of phone calls from wives of doctors looking for them. Most of the time, the doc had promised to be somewhere but was missing in action," said Lynn. "There was a lot of anger there."

"I heard Virginia scream at him more than once," said George. "I can only imagine being a surgeon is harder than some specialties even."

"Peter was a little late picking me up because an ED patient on his service was in trouble," said Lynn.

"Did you scream at him?" asked George.

"Of course not. I don't even scream at you! I asked if I could help," said Lynn.

"Yes, I noticed. You just poke me. I have to warn Peter about that," said George.

"Did you help him?" asked Dorothy.

"Indirectly. I called Dr. Becky to help him with the cardiac problem the patient was having. Between the two of them, they saved the patient and got him to surgery."

"Virginia is an interior decorator. She and Peter hit it off because of their love of art. She has no clue about medical practice," said George. "You do."

"And somehow, Lynn, I don't see you having a lot of issues with a busy doctor. You are a very independent woman with your career and plans to go to graduate school. He'll be lucky if you miss him," said Dorothy, smiling.

"Thank you, Mom. You might be right," said Lynn. "Okay, George, what about quirks? What else do you know about Peter that I should know?"

"I know the ladies like him, but he's a one-woman guy. He makes commitments and keeps them. There is one thing—he sometimes gets into funks," said George.

"Funks? You mean depressive episodes?" asked Lynn.

"I like funks better—sounds less clinical. I remember not too long ago, Peter lost a young patient during surgery. He was a teenager who got severely smashed up in a car accident. He kept going over and over in his head what else he could have or should have done," said George.

"Oh, yes, I remember that case. Peter felt terrible. We talked a lot about it. I think he even took an extra day off to recoup. He never takes an extra day off," said Lynn.

"This may be a naïve perspective, but I think many docs don't make much of an emotional investment into their patients to protect themselves. That's not Peter," said George.

"I agree, especially with kids. He is so great with them, but he pays the price if anything terrible happens to them that he thinks he could have or should have prevented," said Lynn.

"That's all I've got about, Peter," said George. "I think he's a hell of a guy. As long as you don't poke him, you'll be great together."

Lynn, of course, gave George a good poke.

57

Finishing the Paper Star Story

"Do you have time to stop at the house and finish reading *The Paper Star* story?" asked George in the elevator. "They have been bugging Angie and me. Bernie remembers the story, although he's been persistent about hearing the end. The girls are so excited to hear what happens to Tyler and the pink bike!"

"Sure. I've been carrying the book around with me just in case I had a chance to see the kids."

The three kids and Lynn cuddled up on the guest bed Lynn had used before buying her house. She loved looking at their eager faces. She started the story.

"The Paper Star, continued," said Lynn.

Soon the calendar noted it was the day before Christmas. His mother had prepared a spaghetti dinner for Christmas Eve with the promise of a turkey for Christmas Day.

"Mom, that was a wonderful dinner," Tyler had said after eating the spaghetti. Everyone at the table turned to look at him. "What? Why's

everyone looking at me? I'm just being appreciative 'cause Mom works hard making good dinners for us."

"Thank you, Tyler," his mother had said, her eyes starting to tear. "That's a wonderful gift you just gave me."

The family was quiet for a moment, and then the usual cacophony ensued until the DVD of the "Christmas Carol" started up. It had long been a family tradition on Christmas Eve to watch the transformation of Ebenezer Scrooge from miser to philanthropist.

"So, Dad, were there a lot of poor people when Tiny Tim lived?" Tyler asked when the movie was over.

"Yes, Tyler. There were many poor people in England during the times' Dickens wrote the story you just watched. Simply put, he thought the wealthy should do more to help the poor, who were often put in debtors' prisons or horrible poor houses. Even children your age worked in factories and mills under awful conditions to help their families survive."

"I'm glad we don't have to do that," said Tyler.

"You can thank men like Dickens and other social reformers who tried to make the world a better place. So, why all the questions?" Martin Baranowski asked.

"I'm thinking about all these organizations that get presents for kids for Christmas. They're trying to make the world better, right?"

"You got it, son. They do a lot of good." Martin glanced at his watch. "How about going to bed now? It's getting late. You don't want to be awake when Santa comes down the chimney, do you?"

Tyler laughed. It had been a while since anyone in the house believed in Santa. Instead of dreaming of sugar plum fairies, his sleep that Christmas Eve included images of ghosts riding pink bikes.

The next morning, his first awareness when he entered the living room where the Christmas tree stood was the absence of a bike.

"Tyler, what's the matter?" his dad asked.

Tyler was close to tears and couldn't speak. No bike for Christmas.

"Come see what Santa brought you," his mother said. Tyler picked up a baseball glove under the tree that he had his name on it.

"Thanks, Dad and Mom," he said, noticing the glove was from them. It was a used glove but in excellent condition. He liked the glove, but his disappointment from not getting a bike overcame any happy feelings. He went on to open a big box that he'd bet contained a coat. Please, please, he said to himself, don't be green or some other weird color. He exhaled with relief to see this navy jacket from LL Bean.

"Let me see, Tyler," his mother said. "Try it on." Tyler modeled his new coat with great pride. "It's great—just a little big so that you can wear it for a while."

Tyler watched as his brothers opened their gifts. No weird or embarrassing presents for anyone. He noticed his brothers got at least three presents from the people who took their names. He only got a coat, but it was a nice one.

"Mom and Dad, thanks for the glove. It's great," Tyler said. "I'm pretty tired, though. I think I'll go back to bed for a while. I might feel better later." Tyler needed to be alone for a while. He didn't want anyone to know how sad he felt.

"There's still one more present for you, Tyler. Dad went to get it," said Tyler's mother.

Tyler couldn't believe his eyes. His father came into the room, pushing a black and gold BMX boy's bike with a helmet dangling from the handlebar. The colors were bright, the tires full and firm, and every part of the bike was shiny.

"Tyler, say something," said his mother. "You looked shocked."

"Is that really mine?" Tyler asked.

"It's all yours, son. Want to take it for a spin?" asked his father.

Tyler put on his new coat and road his new bike all over the neighborhood. He was sure someone would come and say it was all a mistake and he had to give back the bike and the jacket. He was savoring every minute he could.

"The woman who got your name, Tyler, left a note," his mother said when he finally came back inside. "She said she thought it was better to spend the money she had put aside for your gifts on a better jacket and bike. She was sorry to only give you two things on your list instead of three."

Tyler just looked at his mother in disbelief. "What?" he said. "She was sorry not to be able to do more? I'll go write a thank you note to this woman right away."

"You can't, Tyler. All the gifts are anonymous," said his mother. "There's no way to get in touch with the people who give out the gifts. It for sure would be helpful for her to know how pleased you are. Part of what makes people happy about gift-giving is the smile on the person's face getting the gift.

The next day Tyler and Tommy rode their bikes to the mall. Tyler secured his bike in the rack and polished off a small smudge on the back fender with the elbow of his jacket.

Tyler and Tommy walked over to the Christmas tree that once held all the paper stars with their names. It lacked life now that it was empty.

"Tommy, I've got an idea," whispered Tyler.

"Oh, no, not another one. Remember the time you had the idea of us riding our bikes on the log over the creek? Thank goodness, Les stopped us."

"No, it's nothing like that. First, let's go to Walmart. I know exactly what I'm going to buy," said Tyler.

"Are you sure this isn't going to be dangerous?"

"No danger, just doing something appreciative," replied Tyler.

"Appreciative? What are you talking about?"

"Come with me and learn, buddy. Come and learn," said Tyler, a hint of satisfaction in his voice.

When at the tree, Tyler took out a white tag dangling from a string from the bag he had purchased. On the label, he wrote.

"This note is to the lady who bought Tyler a jacket and a bike. Thank you! The bike is the best bike ever. The jacket fits great, and the color is excellent.

I hope you had a Merry Christmas, too.

Tyler Baranowski"

Tommy caught on. Two thank you tags now dangled from the tree. Tyler left the bag of the remaining twenty-three tags near the tree if someone else wanted to write thank you notes.

The next day, Tyler and Tommy checked on the tree; they counted ten more tags. Every day more notes were up. The tree gleamed from the silver around the tags sparkling under the lights in the mall.

"Tyler, look at your tag. There's some writing on it."

"Of course, there's writing on it, dingy. I wrote on it."

"No, no. Someone wrote more stuff!"

Tyler checked his tag. Sure enough, someone had added something.

"Tyler, You are very welcome! I appreciate you telling me you liked the bike and the jacket. It was kind of you to write. Merry Christmas!"

"The lady saw my thank you!" Tyler shouted. "She saw it." Tyler and Tommy checked some of the other tags. Sure enough, others had other writing on them from the gift-givers.

"It's happening, Tommy. I changed something for the good. It's not a big thing, but people are happier."

"What's with this change stuff? You're not getting weird on me, are you?"

"Come on, and I'll buy you a soda. Do you know that story, "A Christmas Carol"? Well, Dickens, who wrote that story, was into social reform. What we did was not big stuff, but we created something new, we helped people be a little happier, but that's not the big lesson from all this."

"There's more?" Tommy asked.

"Yep. The real lesson is when we are adults, and in a position to help someone else in need, we do that. We don't hesitate. That's the big lesson the people who gave us presents taught us.

"I get that," said Tommy. "But where are we going to school? What kind of jobs are we going to get?"

"Let's discuss our futures over that soda I promised you."

The End

The three kids jumped off the bed and ran into the living room where George and Angie were watching TV.

"Can we go to the mall and get a paper star off the tree?" asked Bernie.

"Can we, can we?" chimed Eloise and Edison.

"We want to get Tyler a present," said Eloise.

"I'll tell you what," said Angie. "We will check where City Hall is putting the list of names of kids who need toys, and each of you can pick a name."

"I think Tyler is grown up by now, but I'm sure there are other boys and girls who could use some Christmas presents. Maybe Aunt Lynn would like to come with us," said George.

"I'd be delighted," said Lynn.

58

Wan and Stan

"Lynn, come quick. We need your help," shouted Beatrice. Lynn ran to the trauma room where Beatrice was waving to her.

"This young woman just came in. She's beaten up pretty badly. Dr. Thomas is in there with her and one of the residents. We are managing her, but you see that older woman standing right there; she keeps trying to get into the room."

"Got it. I'll take care of her," said Lynn.

"Hi," said Lynn. She immediately recognized her as the manager of the nail salon. "Come sit with me over there," directed Lynn.

"No, no. I must stay with Wan," she said. Lynn was shocked to learn the young patient was Wan.

"Are you related to Wan?" asked Lynn. "What is your name?"

Lynn was gently but firmly holding her arm during this time and moving her toward the bench down the hall.

"My name is Long Phan. Wan works for me," Mrs. Phan said. "I see you in the nail salon, too."

"Yes, I use your nail salon. My name is Lynn. Tell me what happened to Wan," Lynn asked.

"Customer no like her nails. She beat on Wan," said Long. "I stopped the beating but lots of blood on Wan. I bring her here."

There wasn't a nanosecond that Lynn believed Long's story. Lynn called the policeman, Frank Romano, who was on duty in the ED that morning, over.

"Stay with her, please, Frank. Don't let her leave," Lynn said to the policeman. "I'm going to check on the woman she brought in."

Lynn raced down the hall to the trauma room. Wan was unconscious but breathing on her own. That was a good sign.

"Beatrice, tell me what happened to Wan," said Lynn.

"How do you know her name?" asked Beatrice.

"Wan is a manicurist at the nail salon I use. The woman who brought her in manages the salon. Her name is Long Phan. What kind of injuries and bruises are we looking at here?" asked Lynn.

"Wan has been unconscious since arriving. We think it's from blood loss, maybe internal bleeding. Vitals are just borderline—ninety-four over sixty and a pulse of eighty-eight. We ordered a blood type and crossmatching. In the meantime, she's getting IVs of Ringer's solution." Beatrice took a deep breath and continued.

"She's got bruises on her upper arm, chest, abdomen, and back. It looks like she might have been hit with a soft but painful object, like a wet towel. Whoever did this to her was extraordinarily strong. There are cuts all over her, some pretty deep; a sharp object might have caused some," reported Beatrice.

"What makes you think she's got internal bleeding?" asked Lynn.

"When we examined her, she winced when we touched her abdomen, which is distended. There's also bruising around her navel and blood in her urine. We had an x-ray done here, which the docs are examining now."

"Here come the docs," said Lynn.

"Let's go, guys. We are taking her to the OR. Blood is ready. Let's get her there quickly," said Dr. Thomas. "Looks like a ruptured spleen."

Lynn called Stan.

"Detective Gregowski. How can I help you?" asked Stan into the phone.

"Stan, it's Lynn. You know the girl in the nail salon you agreed to investigate? She just came into the hospital and all beat up. She's on her way to the OR," explained Lynn.

"Who's the cop on duty today in the ED?" asked Stan.

"Frank Romano," answered Lynn.

"Would you give him your phone for a minute so I can talk with him?" asked Stan.

"Detective Gregowski wants to talk to you," said Lynn to Frank.

Lynn couldn't hear what they were saying but assumed Stan was telling Frank to get information from Mrs. Phan and hold her until he arrived. Frank hung up the phone.

"Detective Gregowski is coming right over, he said to tell you. In the meantime, I'm going to start getting information from Mrs. Phan."

"Great," said Lynn.

Lynn went back to her office to talk with her boss, Claire.

"Thanks, Lynn. I'll alert the administration we might have a trafficked victim in house and that the police are involved. I hope she makes it," added Claire.

"I'll keep you posted," Lynn said.

Lynn was back in her office when Stan knocked on her door.

"Come in, come in," Lynn said.

"I just need to say, you have amazing instincts. How would you like a job consulting for the police?" said Stan.

"Thank you for that, but that makes me think you have some news about that salon and human trafficking," replied Lynn.

"For sure. Molly Peterson did go undercover at the salon. She's so good at this, although I think I've said that before. Wan talked with her about being 'stolen' from her family. Two other girls in the salon are also trafficking victims. We raided the salon this morning, but not soon enough to save Wan from that terrible beating," said Stan.

"Wan is in surgery right now. Hopefully, she'll be okay. It was a terrible beating. I just can't even fathom doing that to another human being," said Lynn.

"That's because you have empathy—these traffickers have none," replied Stan. "Frank also took Madam Phan to the police station for interrogation. I'm here until Frank comes back. You got time for coffee?" Stan asked.

"Coffee? Did someone say coffee?" said Peter coming through the door.

"Hi, there. Peter. This is Stan Gregowski, a detective with the Deer Park Police. Stan, this is Dr. Peter Fry, head of our orthopedic department," said Lynn. For whatever reason, Lynn felt uncomfortable with Stan and Peter in the same room.

"Stan is here breaking up a human trafficking ring. One of the victims came in all beat up and is in surgery," explained Lynn.

"As usual, Lynn is modest. She gave me the first tip about a manicurist at a local salon Lynn suspected was a trafficking victim. We investigated, and sure enough, three of the young girls there were being held and forced to work against their wishes. We want her to consult with the police department since she has such good instincts," said Stan.

"We all love her, too," replied Peter. "I heard you ask about coffee, so here you are," he said, placing both cups on Lynn's desk. "See you tomorrow?" Peter asked Lynn.

"You bet," said Lynn smiling.

Stan and Lynn continued their conversation with promises to keep each other informed.

"Let's do lunch," said Stan.

"Sure," said Lynn.

58

Peter's House and Daughter

Lynn made her usual rounds and settled in to complete her supply list. A text from Wanda caught her attention

Come on up if you can. Sydney's going home.

Lynn was up on the OB floor in five minutes.

"Hi," said Lucas, smiling. "We're going home. Thank you two for all you have done."

"Thank you from me, too. I know I wouldn't have made it through this without the care I received. I have my book and the information about the AFE Foundation. You guys are the best," said Sydney.

"You getting better is our best reward," said Wanda. "Enjoy your baby and send pictures."

"Are you up for coffee, or have you already had a delivery of some from Dr. Pete?" asked Wanda.

"How do you know about coffee delivery? Yes, I've already had some coffee, but I know I'm going to need more," replied Lynn.

Wanda and Lynn found a table in a quiet corner of the cafeteria.

"Okay, spill. What's going on with you and Dr. Pete? The rumors are rampant. Are you really having his love child?" asked Wanda.

"Of course, there's no love child. Who started that one? We need to work people harder—they have too much time to gossip. Just between you and me?" said Lynn.

"Yes, of course. Whatever you tell me goes into the vault," said Wanda.

"What's with this vault thing. Everyone has a vault but me," said Lynn. "Well, it appears Dr. Pete and I are dating. Tonight, I'm having dinner at his house and will meet his daughter," said Lynn.

"Wow, big time meet the daughter. Remember the days when we met the parents if we were dating. Now it's meeting the children," said Wanda.

Lynn laughed. Wanda's cell phone beeped.

"Later, gator. Another baby is coming into this world. Let's do dinner after work soon."

"You got it! Good work with Sydney. You guys are the best!" said Lynn.

Back in her office, Lynn pulled out her checklist of twenty-dollar recipients.

Theresa—up to date—doing well.

Dorika—need to check on the lawsuit by cousin

Shandra—up to date—doing well.

Lucas—up to date as of today—doing well.

Wan—out of surgery but still unconscious—check again tomorrow.

I need to bring up Dorika and Wan with Stan at lunch, thought Lynn. *In the meantime, I need to finish up here and then home to get ready for my date with Peter.*

Angie had agreed to come over and help her get ready.

Lynn had four outfits laid out on her bed before Angie arrived. When Angie saw them, she laughed.

"A little nervous, are we?" asked Angie.

"Petrified is more the word I'd use," answered Lynn. "This is the part of dating I hate. When Peter and I were just friends, I'd go over to his house without a concern about how I looked and what I wore. Now that the relationship has turned romantic, I'm a mess of worry."

"I get that. I don't think it's the romance part that bothers you. Now that you are emotionally attached to Peter, you have something to lose. I have a feeling you could wear an oversized sweatshirt with baggy pants, and Peter wouldn't care," replied Angie.

"That helps, but in the meantime, help me decide what to wear!" replied Lynn.

"I'd go for the red v-neck sweater with the casual pants. Jeans might be a little too informal. Red is a great color on you," advised Angie.

"Okay," Lynn said, following Angie's advice. "How about my hair?"

"Wear it down but pulled back a little—a friendly but not overly sexy look since you are meeting the daughter."

"How's this?" asked Lynn. She had followed Angie's advice and was now ready to head out.

"You look gorgeous. Just remember, Hanna is the same age as Bernie. They get along great, by the way, and you know how much Bernie adores you," said Angie.

Lynn hugged Angie, and they both left the house. Ten minutes late, Lynn was ringing the doorbell at Peter's home, holding a bottle of prosecco and a batch of brownies.

"She's here, she's here," Lynn could hear the voice of a small child saying.

"Hi. Good to see you as always," said Peter, kissing Lynn on the cheek.

"You must be Hanna," said Lynn.

"What did you bring?" Hanna asked.

"Brownies and a bottle of wine. Which would you like?" asked Lynn.

"I don't like wine, but I like brownies," said Hanna.

"Good choice. Can you show me where I can put the brownies?" asked Lynn.

"Sure, come this way," Hanna said, holding Lynn's free hand now that Peter had taken the wine.

Lynn loved the wide columned entrance with the open dining room on the left and the glass-doored media room on the right. The entrance hall ended at the great room, complete with a fireplace, high ceilings, that opened to the bright kitchen with granite countertops. The wooden furnishings had clean lines with inviting cushions and ottomans.

"Here's our kitchen," said Hanna. "Put the brownies anywhere as long as I can see them."

"Do this table and chair belong to you?" asked Lynn, pointing to the child-size set. "Can I put the brownies there?" asked Lynn.

"Can she, Daddy, can she?" asked Hanna.

"Of course," said Peter, "As long as you don't eat any brownies before dinner."

"I'll just come over and check on them," said Hanna. Hanna took off to another room to watch what sounded like a video of a horse movie.

"Hanna is adorable. So cute that she's going to check on the brownies," said Lynn.

"She's a heart stealer, for sure, just like you," said Peter. "Want a tour of the place?"

"But of course," said Lynn.

"It's nothing fancy, but it's comfortable and all on one level, making it easy to maintain and easy to check on Hanna. The living room is where I collapse every night. We can peek in on Hanna in the den, watching *Free Spirit*, on video. There are four bedrooms. The master bedroom and bath and Hanna's bedroom are on this side of the great room. She has her own full bath, too. On this other side of the kitchen area are a guest room, a full bath, and my office," said Peter.

My favorite place is the Carolina room." Peter opened the patio doors to the enormous glassed-in room with a view of the ocean. There was a divider between the Carolina room entered from the master bedroom and the living room.

"This is gorgeous," said Lynn stepping onto the Carolina room. "What a view."

"You certainly are," said Peter. "I missed not having you around all day." He brought Lynn closer to him and kissed her.

"Oh, mushy stuff," said Hanna, barging in. "I'm hungry. When are we going to eat? I checked on the brownies, too. They are okay."

59

Dinner with Peter and Hanna

THE THREE OF THEM SAT DOWN TO A DINNER OF FRIED OKRA, stuffed flounder, and red rice. To Lynn's surprise, Hanna ate all that was on her plate.

"So, Hanna, I see you like fish and red rice," said Lynn.

"I like fish, but red rice is my favorite. Do you like fish, Miss Lynn?"

"I certainly do. Your dad tells me you are eight years old and in the third grade. What do you like about school?"

"School's okay, but I have a problem there," said Hanna.

Lynn could see Peter smiling. *Something good is coming*, Lynn thought.

"What's your problem at school? Maybe I can help," said Lynn.

"I don't think anyone can help. It's my friend Robert. He likes me," replied Hanna.

"If he's your friend, he should like you," replied Lynn.

"Not that kind of like. Robert likes me likes me. You know what I mean? He whispers to me in school all the time and already sent me three Christmas cards. Mrs. Driscoll doesn't like us whispering in class.

We can talk about school stuff, but whispering is not good. Whispering gets you into trouble," said Hanna.

"Did you say anything to Robert?" asked Lynn.

"Yes, I told him we were too young for a relationship," said Hanna.

Barely controlling a laugh, Lynn asked what Robert said back to Hanna.

"Robert told me he will marry me someday when we are old enough. Miss Lynn," said Hanna.

Yes?" replied Lynn.

"I don't want to marry Robert," said Hanna.

"You don't have to marry Robert. When you grow up, you will get to marry the person you choose," said Lynn.

"Well, Miss Lynn. At least now you know what my life is like," replied Hanna in a voice any dramatic movie star would envy.

"Do you think a brownie will help?" asked Lynn. She was trying hard not to smile at Hanna's serious expression.

"I'll try one. Dad said we have ice cream, too, for a brownie sundae," said Hanna as she scrambled to get the brownies.

Peter had the biggest grin on his face, as did Lynn.

"She's adorable," Lynn whispered to Peter.

"I know, and I thought you would think so, too," replied Peter. "I'll be right back with the dessert dishes and the ice cream."

After Hanna was in bed and asleep, Peter and Lynn sat in front of the fireplace.

"You know I like you, like you, too," said Peter. Both he and Lynn toasted their glass of prosecco.

"I feel the same way, except I'm scared. I'm not good at choosing wisely when it comes to dating. Everyone puts their best self forward at first, and in your case, also your adorable daughter. It takes a while to see the issues that will come up as a couple. When they do become obvious, I'm usually too emotionally hooked to leave even if those issues are bad," replied Lynn.

"I get that," said Peter. "I had some of the same reservations about you."

"Really, what were they?" asked Lynn.

"I know you spend a lot of time with the detective, Stan G. You guys have lunch and dinner together as we do. He's smart and good looking and single, too. I hear he likes you likes you, too," said Peter, laughing a little.

"That hospital grapevine is buzzing these days. But Stan and I are just friends," said Lynn. *At least so far,* thought Lynn. "So, what cured your reservations?" asked Lynn.

"As I told you, my ex-wife got interested in someone else while we were married. But two things happened with you. First of all, when I called to say I was going to be late picking you up for our trip, you didn't scream at me, as my wife would do. You chipped in and helped, even."

"But of course, that's what I would do. I know how hard you work because I see what you do," replied Lynn.

"Yep," said Peter. "But also, the other day, Monday, when I invited you over for dinner, you told me you were meeting Stan at the diner to go over a potentially trafficked victim. You didn't hide or in any way cover up the get-together."

"Sure, because there wasn't anything to hide," said Lynn.

"Exactly," said Peter.

"Soooo, did you know I was meeting Stan, and you invited me to dinner anyway to see what I would say and do?" asked Lynn.

Peter put his head down and whispered, "Guilty."

Lynn laughed.

"I wanted to be sure you would be honest with me. Having you meet Hanna is a big step for me. I don't bring anyone else into her life unless I'm sure that person is trustworthy," said Peter.

Lynn raised her glass, and they both toasted to trustworthiness before they kissed each other.

"I really do like you, like you," said Peter.

"Like you, like you back," said Lynn.

60
Stan

"This is Lynn Price," Lynn said, answering her phone in her office.

"Hi Lynn, it's Stan. "I've got some updates on both Dorika and Wan. You got time for dinner tonight?"

Lynn hesitated, then got an idea. "Sure, do you mind if I bring Dr. Fry along? I was talking to him about both cases, and he's interested in knowing more. Being an orthopedic surgeon, he gets to see suspicious injuries."

"No, that will be fine. Can we meet at the *Public House* around seven-thirty?" asked Stan.

"Sounds great. See you then," replied Lynn.

There was a soft rap on Lynn's door, and Peter entered.

"Anytime you want to change your coffee order, let me know," said Peter. "Did I just hear you mention my name?"

"Yep! You did," said Lynn. "Stan has some more news about the trafficking victims, so I also suggested inviting you to dinner with Stan and me tonight as we go over the two cases we are working on together."

"Do you want me to go?" asked Peter.

"I would be delighted to have you come and meet with us. I wanted to set the record straight with Stan. I don't want him thinking we could have a romantic relationship. I have made my choice," said Lynn, smiling.

"Got it. That might involve a conversation that either won't take place or will be uncomfortable if I'm there. How about this? You go and have your talk but ask him if I can call him if I have a patient with suspicious injuries. That's a good idea for me to be more on the look-out," suggested Peter.

"Okay, will do," said Lynn.

"Want to go with Hanna and me this weekend to find a Christmas tree? Do you have one yet? We can get two and decorate both of them. Hanna will love that," said Peter.

"I am more than up for that. Sounds like fun, "Lynn said. Peter's beeper went off with an urgent call about a patient on the orthopedic floor. "Later, sweetie," he said.

The rest of the day for Lynn was full of paperwork and helping out with patients with severe injuries. Christmastime usually leads to an increase in alcohol consumption with more car accidents. Lynn barely had enough energy to go home and change for dinner with Stan.

"Hi," said Stan. He was sitting waiting at a lovely table near the window. *Very romantic*, Lynn thought.

"Hi yourself. How's it going?" asked Lynn.

"Better now that you are here," said Stan. "What happened with Dr. Fry?"

"Peter was busy. It's been hectic today. These holidays are too much for most people," said Lynn. "Peter did ask if he can call you if he has a patient he suspects of being abused. He had a male patient he told me about whose wife was beating him up. The patient was too embarrassed to go to the police."

"The men getting beat up are tricky. Sure, tell Dr. Fry to call me at any time. Injuries and crimes—both up and ...

Stan was interrupted by an angry Alan.

"Now, I see why you left me," said Alan. He was standing at their table, hands on hips, clearly having consumed too much alcohol already, thought Lynn.

"There's another guy in your life, you cheater," said Alan, his voice getting louder.

"Alan, sit down. You are causing a scene. What will your clients say?" asked Lynn.

"I don't care what they say. I have two million in the bank, so I don't even need my job. I just want you to admit you were fooling around on me," said Alan, still standing and getting louder.

"Alan, this is DETECTIVE Stan Gregowski. He's with the Deer Park Police Department. SIT DOWN," said Lynn.

Now Stan stood up, three inches taller than Alan and at least twenty-five pounds of muscle heavier.

"You heard the lady, sit down, or go away. It's your choice," said Stan.

"You don't scare me—you are just all brawn and no smarts. I can outmaneuver you anytime," replied Alan reaching for Stan.

It happened so fast; Lynn didn't see all the moves. Stan had Alan with his arms behind his back in handcuffs in what seemed to be a flash.

"I'll be right back as soon as I get a squad car to pick Alan up for drunk and disorderly conduct," said Stan. "He looks like he could use overnight in the station to sober up. Would you order me a steak, please?"

"Is everything all right here?" asked the manager of the restaurant.

"It is now," Lynn said. "The fellow who was sitting here with me is a detective with the Deer Park Police. He took care of the loud shouter and will be right back. I can place our orders if the waiter comes back over. Sorry for the disruption."

"As long as you are all right, ma'am. That's what matters to us. Your waiter will be right over," said the manager, Tom Anderson, according to his name tag.

Lynn wanted an entire bottle of merlot but decided she'd do that at home. She ordered a glass of merlot for herself, a cobb salad, and steak, fries, and a beer for Stan.

Why do these things happen to me? she asked herself, sipping her merlot. Then she started to laugh. Who else can say they were out to dinner with a police detective when their ex-boyfriend shows up, creating a ruckus? Then she remembered someone had been taking pictures, possibly videos. She prayed this episode would not make the news. *Thank goodness I had invited Peter to come. Thank goodness he had declined! What will he say when he hears about this? Will that make him think I'm too dangerous to be around Hanna?*

61

Dinner with Stan Continued

Stan was back in about ten minutes. As he headed toward their table, the people in the restaurant clapped and cheered. He was their hero. The manager comped their meals for handling the situation so well.

"You are everyone's hero, including me," said Lynn. "I'm so sorry about Alan showing up like that. I have no idea how he knew I was going to be here."

"I'll have the officers at the jail see if they can find out. He might be tracking you through your phone or possibly putting a bug somewhere in your house or car. We'll find out. Don't worry," said Stan.

"I thought that part of my life was over," said Lynn. "I guess I was overly optimistic."

"He's hurt and angry but not a criminal. A night in jail should shake him up, maybe even enough to stop any stalking or confrontations. Happy to be your bodyguard for a while," said Stan.

"Thanks for that offer," said Lynn laughing. "I hope it doesn't come to me needing protection. Wow."

The waiter served their meals, and they chatted about Stan's children and Christmas.

"What's happening with Dorika and Wan," Lynn asked over coffee and dessert.

"Dorika's case is finished. The cousin agreed to drop the lawsuit for Ambrus's money and turned state's evidence testifying as a witness against his accomplices. He and Ambrus were in on a fraudulent passport ring, working with a group from Hungary and adjacent countries. The cousin will get either immunity from prosecution or a reduced sentence for his testimony," said Stan.

"So that's where Ambrus got that money. I'm glad it's over for Dorika. These have been very tough months for her," said Lynn.

"Wan's tormentors are now in jail with no bail. They should be going to prison for a while. It depends on the level of penalty conviction the DA's office will get. It should be pretty high because Wan is under eighteen, carrying out forced labor, maybe sex, and was severely beaten. Plus, there were two other victims. The evidence against them is irrefutable," said Stan.

"What will happen to these victims? Will they be forced to return to their own countries?" asked Lynn.

"Maybe," said Stan. "Wan has a relative in New York City. If they vouch for her and provide her a place to live, she might apply for some sort of visa. She was physically grabbed from her family in Vietnam, so she might want to go back to be with them."

"At least both Dorika and Wan are free from being abused. I hope they can recover from these experiences and find happiness," said Lynn.

"Happiness can be elusive these days," said Stan.

Lynn was about to talk to Stan about Peter when she heard a familiar voice.

"Are you all right?" asked Peter, pulling a chair up beside her. "Hi, Stan," Peter said. Peter was holding Lynn's hand as tight as he could without hurting her.

"The TV news carried the story about a confrontation here. Stan's picture was included leading a man in handcuffs out the door."

"It was just Alan, causing a commotion. He took a threatening step toward Stan. Big mistake. I've never even imagined a detective being able to handcuff someone that quickly. He's the hero of the hour," said Lynn.

"Thank you for protecting Lynn. Maybe you could give me some lessons on how to defend her if something like this happens again. That's the price I might have to pay for being in love with this beautiful woman," said Peter.

Relief came over Lynn like a soft, warm blanket. Peter just saved her from an awkward conversation with Stan. She cherished their friendship and thought rejecting him as a potential suitor might interfere with them being friends. She was pleased and relieved Peter did not see this confrontation with Alan as a red flag about their relationship. He quickly stepped up to wanting to protect her, no matter what.

He's a good guy, thought Lynn. *George was right.*

62

Christmas Tree Shopping

IT WAS SATURDAY MORNING WITH A WEEK LEFT BEFORE Christmas. Lynn had worked the Thanksgiving holiday, so she had Christmas and New Year's off. Today was tree shopping and decorating day with Peter and Hanna. George was buying a tree for Dorothy, which they were going to decorate tomorrow. George invited Peter and Hanna to his house for dinner and tree decorating tomorrow.

OMG! thought Lynn. *I hope everything goes well.*

Peter and Hanna were at the door.

"Miss Lynn, Miss Lynn. We are here," said Hanna through the door.

Lynn opened the door, and Hanna rushed in. "Can I see your house? Do you have any toys?" Hanna asked.

"Of course, you can see the house. Come on, I'll take you on tour. Can I give your dad a kiss and a hug first?" asked Lynn.

"Okay, mushy stuff first," said Hanna.

It was a kiss full of laughter for both Lynn and Peter.

Lynn did the house tour saving the basket full of toys in the TV room for last.

"You have a basket full of toys, Miss Lynn. You didn't tell me about that," said Hanna.

"Take a quick look, and then we need to go get the trees. We will be back here to decorate Miss Lynn's tree later. You can play with those toys then, okay?" said Peter.

"Okay," said Hanna agreeing reluctantly.

"I like this one," said Hanna. She was pointing to a gorgeous balsam fir tree. It was about eight feet tall, but Peter's big room could easily handle it. Peter had the fellow working the tree lot tag and wrap it.

"Now, we need to find a small tree for my house," said Lynn.

"Are you sad to only get a small tree, Miss Lynn?" asked Hanna.

"I'm okay with a small tree. Being small makes it easy for me to take care of it," said Lynn.

"If you need to see a big tree, you can come to my house any time," said Hanna.

Peter is smiling in the background at this conversation. Not only is Lynn in love with him, but his daughter has etched a lovely place in her heart.

"Thank you, Hanna, that is very nice of you to say that," said Lynn.

They delivered Peter and Hanna's tree first.

Peter started with the lights, and then all three of them put up ornaments.

"I like this ornament," said Hanna. She was holding up a reindeer ornament. I think Santa likes it, too."

Lynn stepped back for a minute to watch Peter and Hanna put up the ornaments and then the tinsel. She felt a little like an intruder and couldn't help but wonder about other Christmases when Peter's wife had been here doing this. She then realized she hadn't asked Peter if this was a new house or one he had shared with his wife.

"The tree looks beautiful," said Lynn. "Great job."

"It's the happiest I have been putting up a tree in a long time," said Peter. "Thank you for being here."

"Can we go to Miss Lynn's house now?" asked Hanna. That toy basket had sparked her curiosity.

"Not only can we go to Miss Lynn's house now to decorate her tree, but we can stay there and have pizza for supper. How does that sound?" asked Peter.

"Are there brownies at Miss Lynn's house?" asked Hanna.

"Miss Lynn told me she had something special there for dessert that you can help her make. It's a surprise."

"But I like brownies," said Hanna.

"I think you will like the surprise just as much," said Peter.

Hanna was not convinced, but she knew the toy basket was there, and the pizza was coming.

The small white fir tree Lynn and Hanna, of course, had picked out looked lovely in Lynn's living room.

"Tell me about this ornament," said Hanna.

"That is a replica of my first car. My father bought that for me one Christmas."

"Who is this a picture of?" asked Hanna.

"Those are my niece and nephews. I think you know Bernie. This one is Eloise, and this one is Edison."

"I do know Bernie. I like Bernie, but not like him like him," said Hanna for clarification. "So, you are Bernie's aunt?"

"Yes, Bernie's father is my brother," said Lynn.

"I don't have a brother," said Hanna.

Lynn had to think about what to say about that.

"That's the way it is sometimes. Some people have brothers; some people have sisters; some people have lots of cousins who are like brothers and sisters. As long as you have people who love you, that's what counts. How or if they are related doesn't always matter much," said Lynn.

Hanna was deep in thought. "So, if you and Daddy got married and had a baby, then I would have a brother or a sister, right?" asked Hanna.

"Sounds like a good plan to me," said Peter, chuckling.

"Should we check out the toy basket? We can bring it in here," said Lynn.

Peter delivered the toy basket to the living room. Hanna was immediately enthralled.

"Thank you for today," said Peter. "It was terrific for both of us. The holidays have been tough since the divorce, but today both Hanna and I were happy."

"There is more happiness to come," said Lynn. She turned on the oven and brought out the dough for gingerbread men she had made earlier this morning.

"Who wants to make gingerbread men?" asked Lynn.

"Me, me," said Hanna running to the kitchen carrying Eloise's favorite alpaca stuffed animal.

The three of them baked and decorated the gingerbread men.

"Tomorrow around two, I'm going with George to pick names of kids who need Christmas gifts off the tree in the mall. Do you have any interest in coming with Hanna?" Lynn asked Peter after they made the gingerbread men. Hanna was eating one of hers. There was a bag of gingerbread men for her to take home, too.

"I don't think we have ever done that. I don't know if Hanna would understand what that's about," said Peter.

"I have a book that George's kids ask me to read every year. It's about a sixth-grader whose father lost his job. The boy's first name and those of his brothers are on paper stars with Christmas present requests for the first time. It's poignant and funny at the same time. I'm happy to read some of it to Hanna, and you can finish reading it tomorrow. It's a little long," said Lynn.

"Sounds good. I'll see how it goes over with Hanna. If I don't see you then, we will see you at George's house later. Looking forward to seeing your mom's reaction to her surprise," said Peter. "Hanna, would you like Miss Lynn to read you a story?"

"Okay," said Hanna.

Still carrying the stuffed alpaca, Hanna cuddled up to Lynn on her couch with Peter sitting opposite them. Lynn stopped right before Christmas morning comes up in the story. It was getting late.

"What happens next, Miss Lynn? Does Tyler get his bicycle?" asked Hanna.

Peter did a thumb's up sign about the story.

"It's getting late, and we need to head home so you can get some sleep. I'll read you the rest of the story tomorrow morning after break-fast," said Peter.

"You promise? It's important to me," said Hanna.

"I promise, especially now that I know it's important to you," said Peter, taking the book from Lynn.

Fortunately, Hanna was sleepy enough to leave the alpaca. Lynn now knew what to buy her for Christmas.

63

A Trip to the Mall and Dinner at George's

LYNN WAS UP EARLY TO ORDER AN ALPACA STUFFED ANIMAL for Hanna. She did find one that was a lot like the one in her toy basket but not exact. Fortunately, it would arrive two days before Christmas.

"Good morning," said Lynn recognizing Peter's phone number.

"Good morning to you, too. Hanna's all in to go to the mall today to pick out a paper star. After I finished reading Tyler's story, she stood up with her hands on her hips and said, 'Dad, it's important to me that we get a paper star.' I couldn't resist. We will meet you there at two o'clock," said Peter.

"I'm glad to see you both there. Also, so you know, I ordered a stuffed animal for Hanna for Christmas. Does she still believe in Santa Claus?" asked Lynn.

"I think she waivers a little but questions him being real. She complains he wouldn't fit down most chimneys with his big belly," said Peter. "She's very practical."

"She is so precious. Okay, we will see you at two," said Lynn.

At the center of the mall was an enormous Christmas tree with multiple paper stars on it. George, Angie, and their children were already there when Lynn entered the mall. Lynn could see Peter coming with Hanna from the side entrance. She waved.

"How's it going?" Lynn asked.

"Bernie found a boy his age, Wilson, who wanted a bike, a helmet, and some socks. Bernie wasn't thrilled about socks but is happy to go looking for a bike for Wilson. Edison found a little boy who wanted a Thomas train set. Eloise wants to get a little girl who wants a dollhouse, as she does. We are still looking for that one," said George with Angie agreeing.

"Here comes Peter with Hanna," said Lynn. "No funny stuff, George."

"Me? Funny stuff with Peter?" responded George.

"Hi, Buddy," George said to Peter. "Lynn says we can't do any funny stuff."

"No, I said you can't do any funny stuff. Peter, I trust to behave," said Lynn.

"You still don't know him that well. You wait and see. He's as bad—no, worse than me," said George.

"George, things are going well with your sister and me. Let's not pull pranks yet," said Peter, as they did their weird handshake.

"Hanna, for what little girl would you like to get a present?" asked Lynn.

"Hmm. I'll need to check them out, I think," said Hanna.

Everyone was on the hunt for someone who wanted a dollhouse and someone to whom Hanna could relate. Eloise discovered the dollhouse request. Hanna found an eight-year-old girl who wanted a lovely doll, doll clothes, and a dress for her.

"Dad, can we go shopping for the doll and the clothes now? It's almost Christmas," asked Hanna.

"Okay," said Peter. "We are already here at the mall."

Off they all went looking to fulfill the Christmas dreams other kids had.

George, Angie, and their children left to get ready for dinner. Peter and Hanna went home to wrap presents. Lynn went home to change and pick up the cheesecake and strawberries she had made. She was in charge of bringing Dorothy to George's house, where she and George had her surprise.

"Are we ready?" asked George of Lynn.

"I believe we are," Lynn replied.

"Mom, are you comfortable? We have a little surprise for you, but it will take a few minutes to see it all."

"Okay, but I'll let you know if I get tired," she said.

George turned on the television and inserted a disk.

"Mom, you are responsible for starting the Pocket Full of Twenties Club. This year's recipients and those who helped them out want to wish you a Merry Christmas. I had told you about them, but now you can see and hear them. They all sent videos that George put together as a movie-like presentation. Here you go," said Lynn.

All the participants: Theresa, her husband, and son; Dorika and her new boyfriend, Randy; Shandra and her husband near their moving van; Lucas and his wife, Sydney, who looked great; and Wan filming from her hospital bed, well on the way to recovery. Wanda, the ER staff, Stan and his son and daughter, Molly, and Peter, all sent videos. They all wished Dorothy a wonderful holiday and sent appreciative support for helping so many people every year for twenty years, calling her a great lady. Lynn noticed the way Stan and Molly were standing next to each other on the video. *Maybe there are some romantic leanings there,* she thought. She was happy for Stan.

"I don't know what to say," Dorothy commented with tears in her eyes. "I was always happy to do it while I could. Thank you, Lynn, for carrying on that tradition. Thank you, George, for pulling this together."

Hanna ran up to Dorothy and said, "I think you need a hug," and gave her one.

"Dinner is ready," said George. He poured a glass of champagne for the adults and ginger ale for the children.

George gave this toast.

"I wish the warmth of home and hearth, the cheer and goodwill of family and friends, and the hope of fun pranks to you all."

"George!!!" said Angie, Lynn, and Dorothy in unison!

The End